To Tame a SCOUNDREL'S *Heart*

A Waltz with a Rogue

COLLETTE CAMERON

Blue Rose Romance®
Portland, Oregon

Sweet-to-Spicy Timeless Romance®

TO TAME A SCOUNDREL'S HEART
A Waltz with a Rogue
Copyright © 2016 Collette Cameron
Cover Design by: Teresa Spreckelmeyer

Blue Rose Romance®
8420 N Ivanhoe # 83054
Portland, Oregon 97203

ISBN Paperback: 978-1944973148
ISBN eBook: 978-1944973155
www.collettecameron.com

"God, I love you so desperately, so absolutely,
and this vulnerability terrifies me."

"Beautiful chemistry...You'll cheer for
these star-crossed lovers."
Christi Gladwell USA Today Bestselling Author

Dedication

For B

Beautiful and Beloved

Acknowledgements

A special shout out to Lady Katherine Bone for all of her help with pirate language and to my Beta quintuplets: DF, JH, LB, MD, and JM.

You ladies always come through! I love you!

I must also thank my street team, Collette's Chéris, for helping choose TO TAME A SCOUNDREL'S HEART'S title and for suggesting names for Dominic's Aunt, Miss Sweeting.

You, my dear readers, are the reason I write.

xoxo

Collette

January 1819

Richmond, Parish of Kingston Upon the Thames, England

Bother and blast. Charitable intentions gone straight to Hades and scorched to ashes.

On all fours, Katrina Needham peered beneath the ugly-as-sin floral, chintz-covered couch, and in the process, snagged a hairpin on its braided edge. Several tendrils tugged loose, and an exasperated noise escaped her when the strands flopped across her forehead and eyes.

The sofa's colors—somewhere between sickroom tosspot and stall muck—made her faintly nauseated.

Or perhaps the potent fragrance hanging heavily in Miss Sweeting's overly hot parlor triggered Katrina's uncharacteristic queasiness.

A spicy-earthy scent permeated the stifling room, and, sweeping her hand behind the sofa, Katrina scrunched her nose in distaste.

Incense?

Yes, there atop the mantel beside an Oriental vase, unbelievably even more hideous than the couch. Heat-wilted blossoms sagged over the vase's rim and drooped against each other in a futile effort to survive the ungodly temperature. Probably the revolting incense too. What could Miss Sweeting have been thinking? Surely she must have an inkling how unbearably warm and *smelly* the parlor was?

Most likely the incense was another exotic gift from the infamous Captain Dominic St. Monté. Despite his aged aunt's adoration, Miss Sweeting's privateer nephew would never claim sainthood, no indeed.

A seducing scoundrel? A well-earned title, most assuredly.

At least according to the not-entirely-disapproving

whispered titters and wistful sighs Katrina had over-heard at numerous *le bon ton* gatherings. One learned ever so many improper—*and delicious*—tidbits by lis-tening and observing. Gentlemen either admired St. Monté's prowess and daring, in and out of the boudoir, or disdained him as a reckless rakehell.

Katrina hadn't a doubt he'd earned his devilish reputation in every arena.

A rare, unladylike snort escaped her, and she shoved a burnished curl out of her eyes while heaving a frustrated breath. How far could the thimble have rolled, for pity's sake? And where had that rotten cat vanished to?

If the indulged, fur-covered, hissing ball of podgy unpleasantness Miss Sweeting called Pretty Percival hadn't waddled his tubbiness across the sewing table, knocking the diamond-encrusted trinket to the floor, Katrina wouldn't be creeping about on silk-clad knees, frantically trying to find the treasure. She must locate it before her hostess put in an appearance and Katrina's hoydenish behavior required an explanation.

"Pretty Percival, my bum. More like peevish,

petulant, spoiled-to-his-stubby-whiskers puss."

Maybe, *please God*, the thimble had bounced beneath a chair or table.

Katrina crawled the few feet to an equally garish chair situated between the fireplace and a shelf laden with gaudy knick-knacks. Miss Sweeting truly possessed the most atrocious taste in furnishing. Ghastly stuff.

Remorse immediately poked Katrina. Given Miss Sweeting's modest finances, everything she owned, including the threadbare carpet Katrina kneeled on, was a cast-off.

If the gold thimble hadn't been a gift from The Saint, she wouldn't have been as concerned. But the valuable bauble's absence—*purportedly* once part of a Spanish treasure—would surely be noticed and distress the already feeble, too trusting Miss Sweeting. She doted on her nefarious nephew, though believing everything he said mightn't be altogether prudent. Actually, not wise at all, considering privateers and pirates were opposite sides of the same coin.

St. Monté, otherwise known as The Saint of the

Sea, according to the twittering elderly spinster, regularly sent her unusual trinkets, *hideous things*, and not once during Katrina's visits had Miss Sweeting, Mama's former governess, failed to display the thimble and various other foreign bric-a-brac proudly. His thoughtfulness and obvious affection for the woman who'd raised him contrasted starkly with his privateer repute.

Katrina patted about the chair's legs before sinking lower and scowling at a lone bunny-sized dust ball snuggled contentedly between a gouged rear leg and the faded wall. No thimble hid there either. Where had the dratted thing disappeared to? It wasn't as if the room was vast or stuffed with furnishings and whatnots.

"Percival, you rotten, flea-ridden hair ball, where is it?"

"I regret," a rumbling male voice said, "I cannot stay for tea today, Aunt——"

Percival yowled plaintively, and Katrina, her pink-clad derrière indelicately raised, froze.

Oh, God no. That sounds like—

"Percy, darling. What is it, sweetums? Nic, do be a dear boy and pick him up for me," Miss Sweeting cooed, her tinny tone frailer than usual. "Come, here. There's a love, my pretty, pretty boy."

Perhaps they hadn't seen Katrina yet, and she could ...

Daring a peek, Katrina met a golden, grinning Adonis's amber-hued gaze. The Saint, devil it. And he most certainly *had* seen her.

His attention fixed on Katrina's bottom, he passed the now-purring Percival to Miss Sweeting, and Katrina swiftly angled to her knees, confident her face matched her gown's rosy hue.

When had Captain St. Monté arrived, and why hadn't Miss Sweeting mentioned she expected a visit from him? Shouldn't he be cavorting on the seven seas, plundering ships, ravishing damsels, doing whatever illegitimate, highborn, swashbuckling—devilishly handsome—privateers without responsibilities or scruples did?

The blasted cat languidly blinked his big brandy—*gloating*?—eyes at Katrina and gave a toothy yawn.

"Miss Needham, whatever are you doing on the floor, my dear?" Sparse gray brows knitted in confusion, Miss Sweeting kissed Percival's head and stroked the thick fat rolls layering his tawny, striped spine.

He arched, and his contented rumblings reverberating louder. Beast.

"Looking for your gold thimble, I'm afraid. Percival knocked it onto the floor, and I've spent five minutes searching for the dashed thing." Katrina bit her lip. Ladies shouldn't say dashed, especially bankers' daughters already under the *haut ton*'s disapproving scrutiny. Not all *le beau monde* members took kindly to hoi polloi infiltrating their exclusive parlors—even gently-bred, refined commoners with vulgarly full coffers.

She scrambled to her feet before haphazardly repinning her wayward tresses. Mama would've tutted and fussed if she'd seen Katrina's bare hands, but better to be caught gloveless by a gentleman than risk soiling her new gloves scuttling about the floor like a beach shore crab. Katrina refused to contemplate Mama's reaction if she saw her daughter, rump in the air,

7

on the floor.

The suntanned god chuckled, a deliciously wicked vibration that hadn't any business coming from a man already claiming his striking looks. He possessed features too bold and rugged to be considered handsome in the classic sense, but as a buccaneer? Well, even her heart dared putter faster for a beat or two. His faintly bent nose and the convoluted scar from left eyebrow to temple marred his countenance, but in a dangerous, roguish way.

Those hadn't been there the last time she'd seen him four—no, five—years ago.

She opened her mouth to ask him how he'd come by them, but instead, firmly pressed her lips together. Ladies didn't ask personal questions of gentlemen they scarcely knew. Most especially gentlemen of questionable standing.

Grinning—he *always* grinned—St. Monté bent and retrieved a shiny spot of something near his scuffed boot. No polished Hessians or Wellingtons for him, but well-used footwear. "Is this what you're searching for?"

His voice's timbre—deep, smooth, and assuredly broiling with amusement—enveloped her, and her insides wobbled peculiarly. Perhaps she'd caught Mama's affliction after all, which surely explained Katrina's dampened palms and queer giddiness.

Contriving a genial smile, she eyed the thimble as she perched on the sofa cushion's tattered edge. How had it rolled clear across the room? She trained her narrowed gaze on Percival.

He blinked at her, a definite smug look about his whiskers.

While she'd been hunting beneath the furnishings, had that devil of a cat been batting his new toy about the carpet? Precisely why, even though her pet name was Kitty, she preferred dogs. Sir Pugsley, her cherished pug, hadn't a conniving bone in his rotund body. He wasn't too bright either, but his devotion compensated for his lack of acumen.

Her head barely reaching St. Monté's chest, Miss Sweeting squinted at the gold balanced atop his long forefinger. "I seem to have misplaced my spectacles again, dear boy, but I believe that must be my thimble.

Is it?"

"Indeed, and none the worse for wear from its mishap." After palming the bauble, he plucked her eyeglasses from atop her lace cap. He gently looped a wire around each ear, and gave her a tender smile. "There you are. Better?"

Such a large, unsophisticated, unacceptable man by the *ton*'s standards, yet so tender with his delicate aunt.

"Much, thank you. I quite forgot I tucked them there. I do that often, of late." Her rasping chuckle ended on a harsh, dry cough. "Did you know, Miss Needham, Nic gifted me the thimble, and it once belonged to a princess?"

So he says.

Pride tipped Miss Sweeting's mouth and frolicked in her faded whisky-brown eyes, magnified owlishly by her lenses. It had been a long while since Katrina had seen her so animated, and chagrin nipped her for entertaining uncharitable thoughts toward St. Monté.

"No wonder you treasure it so," Katrina said. No need to embarrass the dear by telling her she'd mentioned those particulars more than a dozen times prior.

The grateful glance he leveled at Katrina propelled heat to her hairline. Hound's teeth, a fan would be most welcome. Or a walk in the still sullen, frosty outdoors. She truly must be ailing, though she exhibited no other symptoms than feverishness and an uneasy belly.

Or perhaps … No, surely St. Monté's practiced charm hadn't affected *her*?

Silly. Of course not. Katrina wasn't fickle or a hair-brained rattlepate. Besides, she preferred dark-haired, brown-eyed, sober men like her soon-to-be husband, Major Richard Domont. He balanced her overexuberant tendencies.

They weren't officially affianced yet, but before Richard's departure a jot over fortnight ago, he'd vowed he'd wait no longer to ask for her hand. When he returned from his assignment in Cambridge, any day now, he intended to approach Papa, who'd already hinted he'd consent to the match. In a fortnight, at the Wimpletons' annual winter ball, Katrina planned to announce their official betrothal.

She'd already selected the exquisite gown she'd wear, a new blue and white confection, and since last fall when she'd confessed her tendre for the major, Mama had steadily assembled Katrina's trousseau in anticipation of a wedding. As the cossetted—though not spoiled—daughter of a wealthy banker, Katrina had her pick of titled gentlemen, but had followed her heart, set on a love-match like her parents' had.

Truth be told, she'd expected to have married Richard by now. He'd courted her since September, and she'd adored him almost from the moment she'd seen him at a ball, standing beside a column, oh so gallant in his crimson uniform. His official duties often called him away for a week or two, yet she'd never doubted his assurances that he'd offer for her once a respectable length of courtship had passed.

As Miss Sweeting shuffled to her favorite chair, St. Monté cradled his aunt's elbow in his calloused, tanned hand. After depositing the thimble safely on the sewing table, he draped a shawl over her thin shoulders and a rug 'round her feet.

Still cuddling Percival, Miss Sweeting gave the

parlor a cursory glance before returning her bewildered attention to Katrina. "You've called alone today?"

"Yes, I fear I have. Mama sends her regrets. Unfortunately, she's abed with a dreadful cold, but she sent along plum preserves, ginger biscuits, and a new tea blend."

Proud despite her humble circumstances, Miss Sweeting would never have accepted charity, so Mama regularly asked the elderly woman's opinion on everything from sherry to new seed cake recipes.

The Saint really ought to have seen to his aunt's most essential needs, rather than sending her useless, gold-painted, glass-jeweled, garish gewgaws. If rumors held true, he'd made a fortune apprehending ships, so his aunt continuing to live on poverty's fringes rather rankled Katrina's sensibilities. Shouldn't caring for family and loved ones be a person's highest priority?

She indicated the basket sitting atop a gossip-rag strewn oval table. "Mama asks if you would please sample them and give your opinion when you see her next."

"I shall be happy to." Miss Sweeting peered at St.

Monté towering above her. "Are you quite certain you cannot join us for tea, Nic? One cup, perhaps? You arrived late last evening, and we've had no chance to truly visit. We've ginger biscuits, plum preserves, and," she fluttered her blue-veined hand at the hamper, "a new tea. Dalton made bread this morning too, and I believe we've Shrewsbury cakes as well."

Hoarded from Katrina and Mama's visit three days ago—in case someone else came to call. Which never happened. Though the oldest daughter of a viscount's third son, Miss Sweeting wasn't always accepted by Polite Society. She'd never revealed why, but Mama had divulged that the censure pertained to a scandal regarding St. Monté's mother.

Poor dear. Miss Sweeting radiated loneliness. And no wonder. With no one but a maid for companionship and a negligent nephew wont to visit once a year at most, Miss Sweeting would have had no company if it weren't for Katrina and her mother's twice weekly calls. During the Season, when the Needhams resided in London, Katrina doubted Miss Sweeting had any guests at all.

Her expectant expression tweaked Katrina's heart as she resumed her seat and attended to her gloves, straightening the inside-out fingertips.

Skimming his appreciative, too-forward gaze over Katrina, The Saint fished an ornate silver stopwatch from his fawn-and-charcoal-striped waistcoat. "I can spare a few minutes since I'm not likely to complete all my business in London today, and I expect I'll be obligated to lodge there tonight in any event."

"Wonderful." Miss Sweeting beamed and clapped her hands once. "Please pull the bell for Dalton. She'll prepare a lovely tray in no time."

The movement jostled Percival, and he opened an eye disdainfully, sending Katrina a baleful glare. Animals adored her—all except this cantankerous feline.

St. Monté dutifully summoned the servant before returning to stand beside his aunt's chair, his stance wide and commanding. Taller, broader, infinitely more powerful than he'd been five years ago, he focused his tawny, penetrating gaze upon Katrina.

His eyes ...

At once, her spencer and morning gown became

heavy. Cloying. She fanned her flushed face with her hand. Merciful God. Most assuredly, she ailed. Best to depart for home straightaway lest she contaminate Miss Sweeting or find herself confined to bed when dearest Richard returned in … in …

A skeptical eyebrow arched the merest bit over The Saint's hooded eyes.

That was, when her beloved Richard returned next …

A sensual smile, probably designed to assault Katrina's senses, tipped St. Monté's mouth, and his other bold eyebrow arced, joining the first on his tanned forehead.

Devil it, whenever Richard finally returned from his gallivanting.

His posture that of a captain braced atop his ship's rolling deck, St. Monté shifted, locking his hands behind him. His black coat drew taut across the breadth of his preposterously broad chest and bulging biceps.

Not that Katrina had noticed the wide planes or exceptional muscles, any more than his anchored stance that emphasized his strong, buckskin-covered thighs and manhood. Or his finely honed cheekbones and contoured jawline, which fairly screamed rogue.

Knave. Rakehell. Scoundrel.

She *was* ill. Why else did her mind wander like a warbling brook?

Katrina doggedly dredged up Richard's form, summoning the hazy image from deep within her illusive memory's bowels. He sported a powerful physique too, her conscience chastised, while another part, the part quite improperly taken with St. Monté, jibed in an annoying singsong voice, *Not as grand as The Saint, by any means, most particularly his manly parts.*

Oh, my God. Do think of something else, Katrina. Anything else.

Katrina mentally stomped on her ruminations and scrambled for a harmless topic. Lodgings. Yes. Perfectly boring.

Except for the bed part, the irksome voice in her head trilled.

Shut up!

"If you're not a member of any of the gentlemen's clubs ..." Would he keep active memberships when he sailed most months out of the year? "I recommend you seek lodgings at The Steven's Hotel. It's less posh than Grenier's Hotel as well as Mivart's, but officers favor it, and since you're a sea captain ..."

That was where Richard stayed when in London, and he liked the place very well indeed.

"Aunt Bertie," The Saint flashed a neat row of square, white teeth, a startling contrast to his olive skin, "would you honor me with an introduction to your lovely guest?"

2

Katrina flinched at Captain St. Monté's casual request, her pride smarting from the unintended jab his words caused. He'd forgotten her entirely. Erased her from his memory as easily and thoroughly as a gobbled crumpet or a piece of foolscap tossed into the fireplace.

Rather chafed her pride, it did.

His aunt's eyes and mouth rounded, and she halted petting Percival. "But my dear boy, surely you recognize Miss Needham."

Katrina cocked her head expectantly.

No acknowledgment registered in St. Monté's feline eyes.

Rot.

"Daughter to Bridget and Hugo Needham?" Miss Sweeting coaxed. "The banker who advanced you the funds to purchase *The Weeping Siren*?"

Even Katrina's encouraging smile produced not so much as a glimmer of recognition.

Double rot and bother.

Well, The Saint really couldn't be blamed. Surely Miss Sweeting didn't expect her man-of-the-world nephew to remember a bumbling teenager he'd met but once, years ago? Still, it did rather deflate Katrina's self-esteem to be so thoroughly unremarkable and completely unremembered.

Canting his head and narrowing his eyes, St. Monté studied her.

Oh, for pity's sake. She would come to his rescue, though he didn't deserve it and her pulverized pride shrieked in umbrage.

"We met but once, Captain St. Monté. Though that time, you prowled this salon like a great caged cat." Managing to wrest her wayward attention from him, lest he see her chagrin, Katrina set her gloves beside her. This most definitely would be a shorter visit than usual. "I presumed you yearned to return to your schooner."

Like she yearned to quit this room and his keen perusal. Desperately.

Even at one-and-twenty, he'd exuded an untamed, masculine grace as he clawed at his neckcloth and paced his aunt's dainty, feminine parlor. Uncomfortable in his formal togs, he'd shaken his overly long sun-bleached mane, his fern-green, topaz-flecked gaze alighting on Katrina for a disconcerting moment or two.

Still longer than fashionable, his streaked hair suited him, as did his bronzed features and even the whitish scar starkly contrasting his swarthy skin. Each proclaimed he'd lived an adventurer's life, and how much grander that must be than playing cards at White's, ogling horseflesh at Tattersall's, or dancing set after set at *tonnish* event after *tonnish* event.

An envious sigh bubbled up her throat.

"Forgive me, but of course I remember you, Miss Needham. How could I not?"

Katrina's disbelieving, artfully plucked eyebrows

wrestled each other in their scramble to touch her hairline first, and her "Indeed?" rang dryer than month-old bread left in summer sun.

A slow smile hitched St. Monté's mouth. "Though you were still in the schoolroom, I believe, and blushed pink as strawberry preserves each time I glanced anywhere near your direction."

He would recall *that*.

Awkward, gangly, with a horrid propensity for spots on her chin and forehead, but desirous to experience society fuss too, Katrina had been thrilled to accompany Mama to visit Miss Sweeting that day. Captain St. Monté's presence had been an unexpected bonus, and she'd become immediately infatuated, as green girls are wont to do. For a solid year, he'd been the hero of many a romantic daydream.

Very well, considerably longer than a year, but Katrina hadn't given The Saint more than a passing thought since meeting Richard, notwithstanding her biweekly visits to Miss Sweeting. But those musings weren't voluntary. No, indeed. Miss Sweeting, without a jot of compunction, thrust them upon Katrina, regaling her with The Saint's latest exploits and commenda-tions.

How, as a young woman bored stiffer than a fire-place poker with Society and yearning for her own ad-ventures, was she to resist succumbing to fanciful im-aginings?

Eyeing him, Katrina affected an affronted air and notched her chin upward an inch. "I'll have you know, my good sir, I thought myself quite grown up at fif-teen, as do all girls that age."

"Ah, fifteen." Two words that insinuated more. Much more.

She could almost hear his mind clacking away, calculating her age and pondering why, at twenty, she remained unwed. The answer was quite simple really, and rather insipid too. Until she'd met Richard, no oth-er man had toppled The Saint from the venerated ped-estal she'd perched him upon. *He* was to blame for her unmarried state.

Nonsensical twaddle, mooning over and fancying herself in love with the boy-man she'd met but one time. Perhaps the innocent girl she'd once been had truly loved the wild, daring St. Monté, but the woman she'd become idolized her calm, steadfast Richard.

Dalton entered, her shoulders and neck every bit as starched as the pristine apron covering her plain, black gown. Her genial tone and the affection glimmering in her eyes belied her stiff demeanor. "Yes, ma'am?"

"Please take this basket to the kitchen and prepare a tea tray. Nic will be joining us after all." From her delighted expression, Miss Sweeting couldn't have been more pleased if Prinny had taken tea with her. She pointed to the basket then drew her shawl snugger. "Oh, and do add another log to the fire, please. I'm quite chilled today. My stiff bones and the pouting clouds tell me a storm's coming."

Gads no, not another bloody log. Sticky with sweat, Katrina would require a bath when she returned home as it was. Her alarm must have shown, for Captain St. Monté collected a surprisingly charming cream blanket from the couch's humped back.

"Let's wrap another throw around you, Aunt Bertie." He slipped the soft, knitted afghan about her thin shoulders. "I fear your guest is about to melt into a puddle, though I confess, I'm accustomed to much warmer climes, and the heat doesn't bother me overly much."

Of course it didn't. The devil quite enjoyed gallivanting about in hell's bowels. Probably paraded about his schooner's decks half-naked too.

That I should like to see ...

"Thank you, Nic." Miss Sweeting scrunched her nose a mite, still raking her fingers through Percival's fur. "You do appear quite flushed, Miss Needham. Perhaps you should remove your spencer."

And reveal her damp bosom and back? The fabric would cling most inappropriately. "I'm not all that warm. I shall be fine."

As soon as she stripped naked and plunged into an ice bath.

In three strides, Captain St. Monté reached the fireplace and set about poking the cavorting flames into a demure blaze. "There, this should keep you warm, Aunt Bertie, without overheating Miss Needham."

Not a jot of moisture glinted on his face while distinct dampness pooled beneath Katrina's arms and trickled down her spine. Between her breasts too, dash it all. A saturated sponge oozed less moisture than her at the moment.

And there he stood, bronzed and *dry*, the flickering fire illumining his noble profile. When he extinguished the incense, Katrina almost whooped with gratitude.

"Next time, Bertie, love, light one incense when you can ventilate the room well. I wouldn't want you to suffer ill-effects from my gift."

"You're so considerate of me, Nic." Miss Sweeting sank further into her chair and shut her eyes.

A faint frown drew Katrina's brows together. Mayhap she'd suggest Mama have Doctor Cutter pay Miss Sweeting a visit. She'd lost more weight, and her pallor troubled Katrina.

Line's bracketed The Saint's eyes, too, as he scrutinized his aunt.

A droplet seeped onto Katrina's temple.

God help her, but ripping off her spencer and

dumping the vase's water over her head truly tempted. Instead, she withdrew the scented lacy accessory passing for her handkerchief and, the instant St. Monté sauntered to his aunt, swiftly patted her face and scooted as far from the fire as the sofa allowed.

Ladies didn't mop perspiration from their person in front of gentlemen, though why they weren't permitted to boggled. Women sweated too.

Think of something else.

"What brings you to Richmond, Captain St. Monté? Do you sail again soon?" She couldn't very well ask him what ships he planned to plunder next. Or what salacious ports he most preferred.

Miss Sweeting's eyelids popped open. "Oh, dear. You don't know. I'd quite forgotten." She rested a gnarled hand upon his fingers cupping her shoulder. "Nic's circumstances have undergone a rather unexpected and dramatic change."

"I'll say they have." An undercurrent of derision weighted The Saint's flippant remark.

Had his *lettre de marque* been rescinded? What would he do now?

The sea had been St. Monté's life these past four-teen years, since he'd stowed away on a cutter at twelve, and his near legendary exploits traveled High Society's most elite circles.

A fortune nudged open many doors, as Papa and Mama had discovered. Aristocratic by-blows sipped Champagne and enjoyed caviar and truffles side by side with those born on the right side of the blanket. Might The Saint now enter the social fray he'd former-ly scorned?

"May I assume we'll have the pleasure of your presence more often?" Katrina oughtn't to have been so giddy at the notion. Richard wouldn't approve, even if he wasn't overtly jealous. Really, betwixt the two, rough pirate or polished officer, only Richard should've appealed. That Captain St. Monté also did, perplexed her no end.

St. Monté's left eyebrow elevated in a lofty and sardonic manner again.

Did he use that expression when facing the cap-tains whose ships he'd pillaged?

"Some mightn't consider my presence all that

pleasurable," he said, that same mockery tinging his words.

"I beg your pardon." Oddly discomfited, Katrina directed her gaze to her wadded handkerchief, crushing the tormented scrap. "It wasn't my intent to pry."

Burning curiosity piqued, nonetheless, and she studied him through her lashes.

Satire, rather than humor, kicked his well-formed mouth upward on one side. "No need to apologize, Miss Needham, and I must ask forgiveness for my boorish behavior."

"Truly, your plans are none of my concern." But she'd like to make them hers. She might love another, but her fascination with the infamous Scoundrel of the Sea hadn't waned a jot.

"Oh, pooh." Miss Sweeting flapped her bony hand. "Tell her, Nic. No doubt the news has swept all of London by now." A gleeful smile pleated her eyes' wrinkled corners even more. "I'd love to see the faces of those pompous highbrows now, I would. We'll see who cuts whom." She tittered before coughing again.

"Oh, and why is that?" Katrina's attention vacillated between Miss Sweeting and The Saint.

"It seems, Miss Needham, my sire was more of a cockscum than I'd formerly comprehended. Upon the death abroad of my half-brother and stepmother last month, certain information has come to light. Information my father made certain be revealed in order for *his* seed to retain the dukedom, no matter the scandal or disgrace doing so caused innocent others."

All traces of the lighthearted swashbuckler vanished, replaced by a pitiless pirate.

Immobile, hardly daring to breathe, Katrina ceased fiddling with her handkerchief. A frisson—no, more of a chilling shudder, truth to tell—jolted her from shoulder to toe. Only an idiot would cross him.

"What sort of information?" Blast her impetuous, babbling tongue and infinite inquisitiveness.

3

Nic swept her a courtly, albeit mocking bow. "Formerly Dominic Horatio St. Monté, the Duke of Pendergast's bastard eldest son, I am—always have been, it seems—the dukedom's true, legal heir."

Aunt Bertie clapped her hands and laughed. "Isn't it absolutely brilliant?"

Brilliant? Not by half.

Familiar rage-induced restlessness gripped Nic, and, jaw set, he paced the threadbare carpet to the shabbily curtained window before marching the return route. A growl, part frustration and part fury, lurked deep in his throat, choking him. He repeated the journey across the room until he'd reined his ire in a modicum.

Astonishment darkened Miss Needham's eyes from a tropical lagoon's clear, vivid blue to the sea's cobalt horizon before a hurricane, and her lips, more ripe plum than petal pink, rounded delightfully in shock.

"I'd not heard of his grace's and her grace's passing," she said, quietly, sympathy brimming in her eyes. "Please accept my sincerest condolences."

Nic dipped his head. He hadn't grieved, and guilt jabbed needle-sharp darts into his conscience. How could he grieve for people he'd never met? Nor had he rejoiced upon learning the title legally belonged to him.

Unexpectedly inheriting a dukedom and his sisters' potential guardianship splayed him, leaving a gaping chasm he'd no idea how to fill or breach, except with fury. Yet he refused to give Pendergast that power over him. Anger and rage turned a person bitter, ate away until hatred directed their every thought, every decision.

Still, he was woefully unprepared for his new role.

Lacking his peers' polished manners—artificial

though they might be—he claimed but a rudimentary education. Letters and numbers he'd learned at Aunt Bertie's small, square kitchen table, and upon the coarse decks of various ships, he'd mastered three languages, navigation, swordsmanship, and other skills required to captain a ship.

Nic favored rum and whisky to ratafia and wine, an unlaced shirt to a neckcloth's choking embrace, and his women well-rounded and equally experienced rather than svelte, virginal misses likely to swoon at a vulgar oath. He didn't dance or converse well either, and the discomfort his elevated position had already caused rivaled a prestigious carbuncle.

On his arse.

Not that he'd ever personally experienced that particular nastiness, but his first mate, Rhye O'Hearnan, had, and his bony bum still bore the impressive scar.

Nic preferred battling two pirate crews at once rather than finagle balls, parlors, or Almack's. With absolute certainty, he'd make an utter arse of himself.

Miss Needham pressed her pretty lips together, and a spark glinted in her keen gaze. Whether compassion or chagrin or something else, Nic couldn't determine. Noteworthy too, that she'd offered sincere sympathies but said not a word about his new status, which revealed what she valued.

People over position. Another point of admiration.

But, God, how Nic loathed the old duke—conniving, manipulative bugger—and God, how he craved the sea's brisk, salty air spraying his face, tangling his hair—her waves frolicking beneath *The Weeping Siren*'s hull. For his young sisters' sakes, he must relinquish his captaincy and venture into Society. A mélange of outrage, grief, and loathing ensured that a steady surge of bile burned his throat and injustice lashed his soul.

Needing a moment, he strode to the dingy window once more and stared outside. The surly, ashen sky mirrored his bleak soul.

A month after Pendergast had secretly married Nic's impoverished, yet gentle-bred mother and tucked her away in a humble cottage, his scheming father wed an heiress—sweet, plain Lady Sarah Trehmain—for her immense fortune. The lying cull had the ballocks to inform Nic's mother, already ailing from pregnancy difficulties, that their marriage had been a farce. When his heartbroken mother died during childbirth, the duke had pawned Nic off on Aunt Bertie, forcing her to vacate her governess position to care for him, a premature, sickly infant.

Aunt Bertie hadn't complained. Not one single word. Ever. She'd loved and nurtured him with a mother's devotion, and he would do anything for her.

Pride and stubbornness prevented her from accepting the house he'd offered to buy her, as well as the bulk of the funds he regularly deposited into an account for her use. And she wondered where *his* mulishness originated. She'd only accept enough money to live modestly and retain her maid of all work, but she kept the trinkets he sent her, wrongly assuming the knick-knacks cheap, worthless baubles. If she ever comprehended the ugly trifles' values, she'd swoon, but in a financial pinch, they could be sold.

The pittance Pendergast had intermittently sent to provide for Nic had ceased after five years—once the duchess produced an heir—leaving Aunt Bertie as her and Nic's sole provider. His father sired two more sons, each dying in infancy, before Nic's sisters, Lady Daphne's and Lady Delilah's births.

Blister and damn, they weren't even ladies any more.

Silence hung heavily behind him, and summoning an enigmatic smile he didn't feel, he faced the ladies once more.

Miss Needham's curiosity-laden expression begged for an explanation, but she'd not ask the questions no doubt tapping at her teeth and fairly shouting from her bright eyes.

Nic would've wagered on it.

As a wealthy banker's daughter, she'd been carefully, and thoroughly, schooled in decorum and propriety. Yet, an untamed glint deep within her expressive eyes hinted rebellion lay buried within her politesse trappings.

Might as well appease her curiosity.

He flicked an orangey cat hair from his sleeve then plucked another off. "Irrefutable evidence has come forth, proving my sire married my mother before he wed the duchess. Wainwright, his grace's solicitor, produced the documents."

A noise somewhere between a hiss and a gasp burst from Miss Needham. "Good heavens. What an unconscionable cawker! I'd run him through, if I were you. Except, he's already dead. Good thing, the rotting fiend." She shook her head, sheer disgust pinching her pretty face. "Go stomp on his grave then. You'll feel better for it."

Aunt Bertie snickered, really snickered. "Oh, if I were only able, I'd dance a jig, I would."

One knew precisely where one stood with Miss Needham, for certain. Nic found her transparency, honesty, and unpretentious mien extraordinarily refreshing, if a mite outrageous.

He rather liked outrageous. They'd rub along quite well.

"Oh, your poor sisters. Surely they're confused and frightened. Whatever will become of them?" Miss Needham sucked in a deep—most indelicate—breath and tossed a thoroughly crumpled handkerchief on the tea table. Her anxious gaze leaped to Nic's. "Hounds' teeth. Did they even know you existed?"

"No." He shook his head, his hair brushing his shoulders. "But they do now. I saw to that straightaway. As you can imagine, they are in shock and frightened about their futures. That's what their sour-faced governess told me when she met with me at my solicitor's. More likely she's worried about *her* future. As she should, after calling my sisters empty-headed corkbrains."

Holding his chin between his forefinger and thumb, he dipped his head. His hair swept forward, and he flicked the tawny strands behind him. Ought to see about hiring a valet and having his hair cut, except his spirit mutinied at the notion of having the last vestige of his former life hacked away.

"How awful for your sisters. Their governess sounds hideous." Compassion lowered Miss Needham's voice, the huskiness strangely comforting. Arousing too. "If I knew them, I'd invite them to stay with us. We've already taken Shona Atterberry into our home, and I know my parents would welcome your sisters. Is there no one they're close to?"

"No one I'm aware of." Nic ran a finger 'round his collar, loosening the stranglehold. Bare-chested, he might've been accustomed to tropical heat, but not attired in a nabob's fancy togs. And these stiffly starched yards of cloth bandaging his neck, gagging him, had him well on his way to cursing like a rummed-up sailor.

No wonder Miss Needham drooped from the room's temperature.

"Old Pendergast, the stupid fribble, named Collerington the girls other guardian, aside from their mother, and he's contesting Nic's request for guardianship." Aunt Bertie, her birdlike eyes round and worried, peered at him, and anxiety shook her wispy voice as her words reminded him of his purpose.

Protect his sisters.

"I cannot imagine why the duke did such a hairbrained thing, especially when he made a point to reveal my parentage in the event my half-brother, Leopold died without issue. Always thought the dunderhead had room to let upstairs. The duke, that is, though, if rumors hold true, Leopold's candle burned dimly too."

Aunt Bertie tsked and tutted. "But naming that rutting cit their guardian ...? No, no, that won't do. Not at all. Everyone knows his financial situation is windmill dwindled to a nutshell, and he has ..." Her faded gaze swerved to Miss Needham, and crimson skated up her thin face. "*Unusual* habits. Or so I've heard."

Unusual? Not by half. Daphne and Delilah mustn't be exposed to his twisted perversity. Precisely why Nic hadn't time to spare with courtship and wooing rigmaroles.

"I don't give a halfpenny about the dukedom, but I do care about my two motherless sisters, and I'll not have them subjected to Collerington's salacious ways, nor will I cloister them with servants and a fusty governess at Chamberdall Court while I blissfully carry on with my life. Daphne and Delilah are the victims in all this wretchedness, and I'll do whatever I must to protect them and help them heal."

"That is a truly admirable sentiment, Your Grace." Approval shone on Miss Needham's face, but the 'Your Grace' falderal would damn well take some adjustment. Ironic that he, a coarse sailor, should inherit a coveted title, one that most heirs typically received grooming for from birth. For certain, he'd not been fed with a silver spoon nor had his bum wiped with silken cloths.

Dalton clattered into the parlor, bearing a laden tray. Once she'd deposited the tea service on the table before Miss Needham, Dalton asked, "Will there be anything else, Miss Beatrice? Would you like me to pour?"

"Thank you, no, Dalton. I'm sure I can impose upon Miss Needham."

"I should be happy to." Miss Needham gave a blinding smile.

And for no reason other than that her sweetly curved mouth stirred a similar cheerful sentiment, Nic's lips swept upward, too, as he claimed the settee's other seat and Dalton took her leave.

Miss Needham set about preparing their tea, her movements graceful and confident. Each shift in position released her subtle scent: floral fragrance, soap, and something slightly spicy.

Cloves, perhaps?

She caught his perusal, but instead of coloring, becoming flustered, or flirting, she offered a swift partial tilt of her mouth and continued her adept arrangements.

Nic spread a serviette on his lap, enjoying her graceful movements

He *had* recognized her.

Instantly, truth to tell, but he'd permitted himself a leisurely inspection of her superbly rounded, tipped-up bottom. Though attractive as a girl, the vivacious woman she'd blossomed into beguiled him, and he didn't enthrall easily. Given his immediate need for a duchess, he'd taken a few moments, probing his memory to recall if Miss Needham had repeated vows yet.

He couldn't have sworn definitively that she'd wed already, which pleased him no end, as did her spirit and obvious affection for Aunt Bertie. True, he didn't stay abreast of the *ton*'s tattle, so Miss Needham might well be betrothed, though her ring finger remained conspicuously bare.

Splendid, and most providential.

He mightn't have to search for a bride after all—not that the task would prove overly difficult. Even if he lacked social graces and had been a rogue of the sea, a lofty title—particularly a dukedom—combined with his deep pockets proved irresistibly attractive to females.

A great horde of sniping, calculating, determined ladies, all bent on the same purpose: snaring a duke and leg-shackling him. Much like the huge ants he'd witnessed in Africa converging on a dead duckling and devouring it, the *tonnish* misses wouldn't be deterred in their quest to become the next Duchess of Pendergast.

A horrified snarl nearly escaped Nic's tightly meshed lips. God help him. Forced to endure the company he'd always eschewed.

After expertly pouring tea, and adding milk and sugar to Aunt Bertie's before passing it to her, Miss Needham lifted the sugar tongs. "How do you take your tea, Your Grace?"

"No sugar or milk, please." He grinned. "Not

many cows aboard ships, so I learned to drink tea and coffee plain early on. The orient boasts the best brews I've ever sampled."

"Mama avows the same. This particular blend is pekoe and congo, but oolong is equally tasty." Lifting her cup, Miss Needham shut her eyelids and inhaled the steam casually spiraling upward. "Mmm." She slowly opened her eyes, like a woman thoroughly satiated after a satisfying tumble, and taking a dainty sip, her azure gaze sought his.

Nic indulged his naughty daydream for a few tantalizing moments.

Miss Needham's sultry eyes questioned him above her teacup's rim. "Now, please tell me about your dear sisters. What do you intend for them?"

Nic reluctantly allowed the tempting image to fade away. "I'm still working on those details."

"Perhaps I may be of assistance," Miss Needham offered. "After all, my parents' sphere of influence is quite substantial."

Direct and straight to the point—no tiptoeing around the issue with inferences and innuendos. Another factor in Miss Needham's favor. Yes, she'd do quite well, and enlisting her help? Bloody brilliant, if he didn't say so himself.

"I'll have to petition the Court of Chancery for Daphne and Delilah's guardianship, and that is more successfully done if I've married and can establish myself as a respectable fellow, rather than a roving, ship-pillaging scoundrel." Nic helped himself to a ginger biscuit, a favorite yet rare childhood treat, as he gauged Miss Needham's reaction.

She nodded, her intelligent face meditative. "Indeed. I understand the advantage. A generous donation to the church as well as a charity or two wouldn't go amiss. Perhaps something to help London's street children? It wouldn't hurt for you to be seen attending services either, though I personally find *le beau ton*'s Sunday form of Christianity galling."

"Sound advice." Nic managed to conceal his cringe. He hadn't set foot in a church since he ran away. For the girls, though, he would and pray he didn't burst into flames directly upon entering the sanctuary.

"Hmph, you're hardly a criminal, Nic," Miss Sweeting scoffed. "The Crown has sanctioned your activities, and only a codspate would dare speak against you now that the dukedom is yours." Aunt Bertie removed her spectacles and, after holding them to the window light, proceeded to wipe the lenses with her shawl's edge. "You needn't rush into a union quite yet. Though I'm certain eligible misses will flock round you like flies to sweets."

The duckling image popped to mind again, accompanied by a violent shudder.

Preposterous, a man of his stature and experience trembling in his boots at the prospect of parleying with eager parents and eligible misses hoping to make a brilliant match.

"No, I think I must enter the parson's mousetrap. For my sisters' sakes." No matter how much the idea appalled him. By God, nothing else would drive him to such extremes. However, he'd not parade before the *ton* on his quest. There had to be a better way.

"How old are your sisters? I confess I cannot remember if I've ever been told." Miss Needham stirred a fresh cup of tea.

"Daphne is thirteen and Delilah eleven." Idly rubbing his scar, he pictured his sisters the last time he'd seen them from afar, their red-blond heads dipped together as they crooned over a dame's fluffy white, beribboned kitten. He'd never been permitted a formal introduction, though he'd requested one multiple times. "With their mother gone, they'll need a woman's gentle presence, and I know naught of young innocents' ways or needs."

Miss Needham coughed into her hand, muttering something which sounded suspiciously like, "Bold truth there."

He grinned. Saucy wench.

"Dominic ...?" His aunt dashed at her papery cheek. Tears? Why now?

Nic swallowed his spicy-sweet mouthful before angling his head.

Aunt Bertie rarely used his full given name. His mouth twitched. Well, she had often enough when he'd been into mischief as a lad, which, given his propensity for adventure and mayhem, had been more often than he cared to admit. However had she put up with his antics? His anger and petulance? His naughty humor? Frogs and snakes and caterpillars in the kitchen and parlor?

He knew the answer, of course. She adored him.

Love covered a multitude of sins, thank God.

"What has you distressed, Bertie, love? My marrying so speedily? I must find a willing bride yet, and that may take a few weeks." She fretted for him, even after he'd proved his prowess as a privateer. That was what normal, loving parents did. What he'd do when he became a father. "What if I promise to allow you input regarding the lady I select, and if you object to her, I'll consider another? Would that satisfy you?

After all, he intended Aunt Bertie reside with him, and his wife must treat his cherished aunt with respect. As she must his impressionable sisters. The girls might prove to be a trifle difficult at the onset, and he would insist upon a patient and sympathetic duchess, not a feckless, selfish shrew.

Blast, if Collingsworth weren't respectably married, Nic might wait to venture down matrimony's prickly path himself. "I'm confident between us, we can select a lady who we'll rub along well with."

He wasn't at all confident, but that burden was his to bear.

"Yes," said Miss Needham. "A lady who will adopt the role of a loving elder sister, rather than attempt to replace their mother. They'd resent that, I think." Daintily nibbling a buttered bread triangle, she considered Nic. A dab of butter remained at her mouth's corner, and she darted her tongue out to lift the trace.

If Aphrodite had manifested from the linen-wrapped teapot's steam, he wouldn't have been able to haul his attention from the moist pillow passing for her lower lip. His own tongue breached his lips briefly before he snatched the traitorous organ inside again.

Nic wiped his moist brow. Less than half an hour in Miss Needham's presence and he'd contemplated bedding her multiple times. Her qualifications and appeal grew by the minute.

"A woman boasting a degree of acumen and wit, too." Gazing into the fire, her eyes half-closed, Miss

Needham tapped her chin. "And not given to vapors or histrionics. Can't abide either, personally. Musical and artistic aptitudes are desirable, as is a strong constitution. And since you've traveled extensively, a well-read lady with geographical knowledge would provide you discussion fodder other than fashion or weather twaddle."

"Absolutely." Nic's hearty agreement earned him a grateful tilt of her lips. Sharp-witted, she'd neatly and concisely described his ideal duchess. Particularly that last bit. By Jove, he'd go mad, listening to bilge-water prattle about bonnets and ribbons and parasols or the latest *on dit*. His duchess must at least be able to carry on an intelligent conversation about something other than fripperies and gossip.

Undoubtedly, Miss Needham would be able to.

Soft snuffling drew his attention to his aunt hunched in her chair.

"Aunt Bertie?" he prompted gently, setting his cup upon the low table this time. "Please tell me what has you distraught?"

She sniffed and dabbed her damp face. "It was

selfish of me, I know, and I've wronged you, Nic. I meant to tell you. Truly, I did."

"What was? Tell me what?" He shot Miss Needham a puzzled look.

Slightly lifting a shoulder, she gave a tiny shake of her head. She had no more inclination what caused his aunt's upset than he did.

"I should've suspected Wainwright possessed evidence verifying Maureen married Pendergast, but I knew you'd be taken from me if your legitimacy was confirmed. And Pendergast, the cur, would've destroyed me—threatened to do so if I questioned him or pursued the issue further. How could I, a poor spinster without means, prove my sister married the duke prior to his and Lady Trehmain's nuptials?"

"You did what you thought best, and I cannot fault you for it, my dear." Nic leaned across the table and took her thin hand in his. "I shall always be grateful for your sacrifice, and I'm a far better man having been raised by you than that spineless sot." He kissed her fingertips before releasing her.

Misery still etched her lined face, and she spluttered into her handkerchief. "I cannot quite recall how, but Wainwright and the late duchess claimed a distant connection."

"And rest assured, neither benevolence nor misguided loyalty motivated Wainwright's silence all this while. I haven't a doubt he blackmailed my father. Wainwright's first letter to me indicated he expected a hefty settlement for confiding the truth at long last."

"Hellfired cull." Miss Needham's teacup clacked violently against her saucer, and tea sloshed over the brim. Using a serviette to mop her spill, she didn't apologize for her unladylike outburst. "I hope you do not intend to pay him a pence."

No simpering miss there. No indeed.

Better and better.

"I do not," Nic said.

"Don't you blame yourself, Miss Sweeting. Papa often warns me about the extreme measures compunctionless people will go to in order to protect themselves. I fear it's not a trait reserved for the highborn." Her hands now folded primly in her lap, Miss Needham slid Nic a contemplative glance and bounced her thumbs together, revealing her agitation, or perhaps, her pent-up energy. "Had you not cared for his grace, he might have ended up a pitiable, uneducated urchin instead of a respected privateer."

His grace. God above, how would Nic ever get used to that form of address?

A log shifted, and the flames crackled with renewed vigor.

Percival hopped to the floor, and after stretching and yawning, pattered to the hearth and plopped his corpulent self before the fire.

A man of Nic's prior profession wasn't typically respected or embraced by the upper ten thousand, not that he gave a damn what that pernicious lot believed. He did, however, care what *she* thought, dammit.

Relaxing against the settee, he draped an arm across the top. Miss Needham's shoulder was but a hand's width away. "Please, when we are in intimate company, Miss Needham, might you address me more informally? Perhaps merely Nic or Saint, or if you must use my new title, Pendergast?" He winked and bent nearer. "Though I cannot guarantee I'll answer to the latter."

"That's not at all proper, as I'm sure you're aware." A sable eyebrow swooped upward as she teased. "However, since I've always thought of you as St. Monté, if you've no objection, I'll address you as such."

"I would be honored." She'd thought of him? How often?

From the pink tinting her face and her sudden fascination with her spencer's buttons, often.

She captured her lush lower lip between her pretty teeth.

Quite often.

Satisfaction burgeoned behind his ribs. Well now. What an interesting, and most agreeable, development.

"And there were the children to think of too," Aunt Bertie said, her tears finally dried.

She prattled on, oblivious to the intense, sensual undercurrent between him and Miss Needham.

"As a bastard—oh, I quite hate that word—poor Nic suffered rejection and humiliation, but he possessed the strength of character to overcome the jibes and ridicule." Aunt Bertie folded her serviette. "Leopold, though sweet, was a soft, weak hobbledehoy. And those darling girls ... Well, I'll tell you, they'll suffer the most from their sire's perfidy."

"And that is why I must wed. To ensure their wellbeing and futures." Nic drummed his fingertips atop the settee's carved wood. "Perhaps you'd consider aiding me in my venture, Miss Needham? With your parents' permission, naturally. I'm not up to snuff on niceties, and my dancing skills are rather rusty."

No understatement there.

Why not make her an offer now? No, she didn't seem the type to rush pell-mell into things. Well, actually she did, but best to woo her for a week or two at least. Make certain she didn't possess an objectionable trait or habit.

Aunt Bertie fairly beamed, appearing perkier than she had since he'd arrived. "What a grand notion, Nic."

Eagerness lent a becoming glow to Miss Needham's already rosy cheeks. "I should be delighted to, and I'm sure I speak for Mama when I say she will be as well. We must start by introducing you to all the eligible misses in the area. No, no, not yet." She shook her head, and the mahogany tendrils she'd repinned tumbled forth once more. Absently tucking them behind her ear, she said, "We need to make a list of what attributes you require in a duchess and what things you cannot abide. That will save time and avoid introducing you to ladies who won't suit."

"But of course." Almond brown hair, blue eyes that change color depending on her mood, an exuberant smile, a penchant for speaking her mind, as well as a sumptuously rounded form topped his preferences. In a word—her. "Since I intend to return to the sea when my sisters are raised and wed, she'll need to be amenable to spending months alone."

Miss Needham's face puckered before she smoothed the delicate planes once more. "Why not take her with you if she's of a mind to accompany you?"

He chuckled and raked a hand through his long hair. For certain, she knew little of sailing. "Women aboard a vessel are notoriously bad luck, and I hardly think my duchess would relish jaunting about the oceans. It's a rough life and not for the fainthearted, let alone a lady accustomed to life's luxuries. Nay, better she stay ashore."

"Hmph, I should think a man and woman dedicated to one another wouldn't want to be separated." She sat straighter, disapproval turning her mouth downward.

Had he riled her? "Aye, but I'm not wedding for love, but rather for convenience, which, you have to admit, doesn't require devotion or constant company. Does that preclude you from aiding me?"

"Oh, flim-flam, of course not. Don't be a goose." She flapped her hand, giving him an incredulous look that suggested he had more hair than wit.

No other person had ever called him a goose. Several other choice words, yes, but never a goose. Miss Needham unquestionably topped his list of potential brides. That business about wanting to be with her spouse might present an issue, but he'd deal with that obstacle when the time came.

"We're having a dinner party, three nights hence.

You must join us. Mama won't object. In fact, she'll be delighted to have such a prestigious guest, and your presence will balance our guest list. We're one gentleman short. That is, we will be if the major arrives by then." She tapped Nic's forearm lightly before attending to her tumbled curls once more. "And naturally, you'll attend the Wimpletons' ball with us as well. I believe there's a soirée and another dinner party before then too."

"The major?" One of her brothers? She had two older ones, if he recalled correctly.

She stopped fussing with her gloriously shiny hair, and graced him with a beatific smile. "Yes. Major Richard Domont, my intended."

4

Katrina stood and after shaking out her skirts, gathered her gloves and reticule. She had stayed longer than she'd planned, after all, but her reasons were most altruistic. On his own St. Monté—no, Nic suited him much better—would botch the business of finding a wife. He was a rather endearing oaf. "I must be on my way, but please do call when you return from London, and we can put our heads together and compile an acceptable list of qualifications for your duchess."

"Don't forget the dance lessons or refresher on protocol and decorum," Miss Sweeting said, almost too enthusiastically, before finishing her biscuit. She tossed Percival a crumb, which he pounced upon with portly enthusiasm.

"I feel like a damned lad in shortpants again." Nic didn't appear half as agreeable as he had a moment before, no indeed. His tawny brows formed a harsh vee, and an assessing glimmer had replaced the jovial glint in his eye.

Had Katrina said something to displease him?

She wracked her brain.

No. He'd asked for her help, and she'd willingly offered it, so why now did he act all starchy and offended?

"Thank you for visiting, my dear. You know how much I look forward to your company." Miss Sweeting angled her cheek for a kiss. "You'll come again, on Thursday, as always?"

"Of course. Mama should be recovered too. I know she's been experimenting with a new scent, so prepare to receive a bottle or two of perfume if she cannot decide betwixt them." As she bussed Miss Sweeting's dry, crepey cheek, concern again inundated Katrina. Miss Sweeting wasn't well. "Would you see me out, Your— Nic?"

Terribly brazen to use his given name, but of all his forms of address, Nic fit him—the man, not the privateer, not the duke, not the brother, or bastard son—simply *him*.

He extended his arm, the coat fabric worn a bit threadbare at the elbow. "It would be my utmost pleasure."

Katrina cut him an arch look.

Goodness. She could almost believe he'd insinuated something more as she laid her bare hand upon his sinewy arm. Not an ounce of fat on him anywhere, she would wager. Did he climb the mast and rigging himself? Probably. He didn't seem the type to leave the dangerous work to his crew while he sat idly by.

She could more easily picture him clinging aloft, his muscles straining and bulging, than circling a dance floor, although, each required a certain form of animal-like grace and carriage, and he exhibited a masterful command of both.

Katrina's step faltered to a stop once out of Miss Sweeting's earshot. She still held Nic's arm and had accidentally brushed against him when exiting the salon's narrow doorway, not that she permitted herself to acknowledge the heat permeating her spencer and gown once more.

Affianced—*almost affianced*—ladies did not notice, and most certainly did not enjoy, a gentleman's attention or touch other than their betrothed's.

"I'm concerned about your aunt." Katrina gestured toward the door. "The parlor is unbearably warm, yet she complains of cold, and her skin is too dry to the touch. I think a physician ought to be consulted, but I know you intend to leave straightaway."

Nic swiveled to stare at the empty doorway, consternation creasing his forehead. "I'll delay my departure. She's too important to me to risk her health by waiting until I return. Can you recommend a physician?"

"Certainly. Doctor Cutter is attending Mama this afternoon. I'll ask him to stop here on the return trip."

"I'd appreciate that. Very much."

Gratitude shone in his genial gaze. He had the most astonishingly beautiful and expressive eyes. He might be coarse and rugged from his privateer life, but within the depths of his spectacular, thick-lashed eyes, humility and kindness lurked.

His willingness to set aside his vocation, for the time being, at least, to care for his sisters touched her deeply. Most titled men of her acquaintance were arrogant, selfish boors concerned only with their pleasures and interests.

After withdrawing her arm, Katrina went about donning her gloves. Once finished, she permitted him to assist her into her pelisse, steadfastly ignoring the rush of pleasure the simple act elicited. The brush of his calloused fingertips at her nape and shoulder produced curious little quivers.

Quivers she oughtn't to have noticed, let alone enjoyed.

Richard possessed work-roughened hands too.

So why didn't Richard's fingers accidently sweeping her skin provoke the same tingling response? Assuredly, she felt tender arousal when he kissed her, but his mild caresses never had the ability to turn her knees custard soft or caused her to want to arch into him. Oh, he'd wanted to do more, had pressed her to do much more, but Katrina had been adamant about having a ring on her finger before she succumbed to passion's lure.

Far past time she wed and experienced the marriage bed. Once her virginal curiosity had been satisfied, she'd not respond like an untried maid when a dashing man paid her attention.

Only one man has ever had this effect on you, Katrina Lorraine Rebecca Needham.

Stubble it!

She was not fast or fickle. She loved Richard. She couldn't wait to be his bride.

She needed to think of something else.

"It's an honorable thing you're doing, Nic. I can only guess at the sacrifice you're making and how difficult it must be to relinquish captaining your ship."

Katrina tilted her head to meet his gaze. She wasn't short, but his height topped hers by several inches. For a man reputed to have seized over fifty ships and taken innumerable lives, he possessed the gentlest eyes she'd ever seen. In the salon, they'd been a mossy green, but in the entry's dimmer light, they appeared more marine, and a deeper forest green rimmed his outer iris.

"I've always wanted to be part of a large family, and I'll admit, Pendergast's refusal to allow me to know my brother and sisters has chafed my ar—that is, my pride." He scratched his cheek, charmingly nonplussed.

Tying her bonnet's ribbons, she grinned. "Never feel you cannot be completely candid with me, Nic. Chafed your pride isn't at all the same as chafed your arse. The duke was a selfish, inconsiderate blackguard for what he did to you, her grace, and his other offspring. You've been remarkably civilized and shown great restraint in a deucedly awkward circumstance. I'm not at all sure I could have been as gracious."

"Has anyone ever told you how refreshingly honest you are, Miss Needham?" Nic chuckled and tucked the curl teasing her cheek beneath her bonnet's rim. "I quite like it." He touched her nose and winked. "I quite like you."

Best to ignore that last bit, though her woman's pride puffed proudly. Gathering her wits, which had scattered about the entry like minute dust particles floating in the sun, Katrina pulled a face. "Yes, it is an unfortunate habit. I've been known to say the most shocking and improper things. Mama tells me it will land me in a scrape one day."

"Well, promise you'll always be entirely straight-forward with me." Nic opened the door, but didn't step through. "When are you to wed?"

Katrina eyed the driver patiently standing beside Papa's carriage. "No date has been set. Actually, Major Domont hasn't asked Papa for my hand yet. He's promised to as soon as he returns from Cambridge." *He's taking his dratted sweet time.* "I expect we'll an-nounce our official betrothal at the Wimpletons' winter ball."

Why had she confessed that drivel? Nic didn't need to hear her personal business. Perhaps he'd de-cided his request to help him find a duchess had im-posed since she was about to marry. The notion dis-tressed her more than it ought to.

"A major in His Majesty's Army. An honorable profession." Nic opened the door. "I greatly admire men committed to serving the crown and protecting Britain."

"Don't you do much the same? I'd vow your vocation is as worthy and certainly at least as dangerous. Probably more so." It astounded her that she meant every word when, an hour ago, she'd considered him and his chosen profession improper. A cool breeze ruffled her hem, and she grinned again. "And I dare say, you've had grand adventures. I should love to hear of them sometime."

Instead of taking her arm, Nic tucked her hand into the crook of his elbow and escorted her down the short flight of stairs. Her hand nestled against his side felt so right, so comfortable, she couldn't object.

Frost dotted the ground where the feeble sunlight failed to penetrate, and she shivered. Beastly hot inside and monstrously cold without. How could a person accommodate such extremes?

"Have you known the major long, Miss Needham?" Nic bent his neck to ask the question, and his breath tickled her ear.

"Since September." Katrina tipped her chin, her

face but inches from his. He *did* have amber and gold shards in his eyes. That was what gave them the yellowish tint.

He scrutinized his aunt's overgrown yard, the sagging fence, and the tilting chimney before lowering his gaze. "A love match, I presume? And of course, he's tall, dark, and ever-so-handsome in his scarlet uniform."

Katrina gave one partial nod, not at all certain the conversation should continue. She didn't want to speak of Richard with Nic. To do so marred the natural affinity that had sprung up between them. Her reluctance to disturb their kinship ought to have her darting straight for the carriage without a backward glance.

Instead, she murmured, "Couples should marry for love, should they not?"

"Aye, whenever possible." Nic smiled, a cordial arcing of his handsome mouth, exposing a dimple in his right cheek. "I'm glad for you. I hope, with your assistance, I might find a portion of your joy." He lifted a shoulder an inch. "Still, I'd be content with a kind, patient, and faithful woman. Even if she doesn't love me."

Katrina gripped his forearm, staring into his eyes and seeing the wounds he strove to disguise: the rejected little boy, the disparaged privateer, and now the disdained duke—at least until he proved himself.

"Don't settle for mediocrity, Nic. Wait for love. Your sisters will be the better for it, and you deserve to be loved for yourself, not for what your title promises."

My, but she'd achieved a new level of audaciousness, advising a privateer on matters of love. No, a duke now, and one most assuredly more experienced in such matters than she. Had he ever loved a woman? She opened her mouth to ask, but this time, common sense prodded her hard. That was much too forward a thing to ask a man who'd been a stranger but an hour ago.

Why did it seem like she'd known him for years then?

"Katrina, you've called me Nic several times now, so I think it only fair I address you by your given name, scandalous though it might be."

Never had her name sounded half so lovely rolling

off a man's tongue. She wanted to ask him to say it again, and again, and again. Instead, she acquiesced with a tilt of her chin. "Only when we are alone, Nic."

He touched her chin with the familiarity of an older, beloved brother. "I'll ponder your genial advice and look forward to calling on you once I've completed my business in London."

Long after Nic had handed her into Papa's carriage, and she'd settled into the comfortable ruby squabs, a lap robe across her knees, Katrina still felt his fingertip upon her nose, heard her name on his lips, and saw his eyes alight with humor. He smelled rather lovely too, and he was a good man, through and through. Despite the challenges Fate had dealt him, he'd overcome them while retaining a rare, soul-deep decency.

A gentleman privateer. No, a ducal privateer.

Before she left the carriage, Katrina had assimilated a partial list of qualifications she believed made for Nic's perfect bride, yet she couldn't summon the name of a single female she deemed worthy to be his duchess.

Late in the afternoon three days later, Katrina sat at her library writing desk, determined to have a list prepared for Nic when he came to dinner. Biting a fingernail and tapping her toes in an unsteady cadence, she deliberated the messy, crossed off *duchess prospectus*, as she'd come to call the list. Over the past hour, she'd scribbled name after name and found fault or exception with every lady she chose.

She barely knew him; so how could she be so certain each of the ladies wouldn't suit?

Still, Katrina stubbornly refused to admit defeat. She'd made Nic a promise and meant to keep it. Who else would aid him if she didn't? More on point, who could he trust not to have an ulterior motive? She was already affianced—*almost*—so he needn't worry she'd set her cap for him.

"Miss Delores Barringsworth?"

Katrina scritched the name onto the foolscap. And promptly scratched it off.

"Too flighty. She'd drive Nic mad, batting her eyelashes, and that horrid giggle ...? Sounds like cats drowning. He'd toss her overboard in a fortnight."

Katrina set the nib to the paper again.

Think.

She'd experienced two Seasons, and since half the *ton* owed Papa's bank money, she'd been accepted into the most prestigious parlors. Well, accepted mightn't be wholly accurate. Tolerated rang truer. *Le beau monde* might abide wealthy commoners, but they didn't embrace them wholeheartedly.

Still, she knew women. A myriad of them. Young. Old. Short. Tall. Slender. Portly. Innocent, fresh-faced, dewy-eyed girls and cosmetic-tinted, sharp-clawed hellcats.

"Surely there must be scores of suitable ladies." Many not altogether pleasant or the least compatible with Nic, however. She screwed up her face and pursed her lips. "Come now, Katrina. Put your mind to the task. In all of England, there has to be a handful of un-objectionable prospects."

She'd intended to have a partial list of acceptable

candidates for Nic tonight, but every time she sat to assemble duchess-worthy females, her mind went emptier than a parsonage's coffers. And then she'd get lost in daydreams of his swashbuckling heroics.

What a dolt. Get to it.

Closing her eyes, she dredged up the last ball she'd attended and the dozens of elegantly clad ladies swirling about the dance floor. Miss Belinda Newcomber? Not with her penchant for tears and whining. Lady Mary Somerton? Hmm. Perhaps ... Bother, she wouldn't do either. Too loud, too haughty, and too confident of her position. What about that sweet, plump widow, Leticia Chapman? No, she'd been moon-eyed over Sir Gibson Armstrong.

Katrina sighed, opened her eyes, and set aside the quill.

This shouldn't be so confounded difficult.

A movement in the courtyard beyond the burgundy and gold brocade panels framing the window snared her attention. Had a dark-haired man passed? Her pulse leaped, and she dashed to the window, catching a glimpse of a deep cherry-red coat disappearing up the stairs.

Richard? At last. He'd returned in time for to-night's dinner, as promised. A few moments later, the knocker sounded, and Osborne's measured stride echoed through the corridor as he strode to answer the door.

Katrina had missed Richard, but her match-making undertakings for Nic had helped to pass the time as did planning her wedding. Also, Mama had several details she'd insisted on discussing with Katrina, admonishing, "It's never too early to begin preliminary planning for such a special event, Kitty, and trust me, my darling, your major will be all the more grateful for not having to trouble himself with such trivialities."

Nonetheless, it seemed somehow premature, even slightly disloyal, not to include Richard in the preparations. Papa assured her the majority of men were content to leave such frivolous details to females to hash out. Hopefully, Richard was one of those men.

Katrina hated to admit it, even to herself, but unease had niggled the tiniest bit when Papa hadn't received his customary correspondence from Richard. Not permitted to write Katrina directly, another stuffy social protocol, Richard typically sent 'round a missive or two and until now, had steadfastly alerted them to his anticipated arrival time.

A glance at the chinoiserie black mantel clock as she smoothed her hair then her simple morning gown earned a slight grimace. Not quite half past four. Too early to arrive for dinner, but perhaps he'd been as eager to see her as she to see him and dared breach decorum. Fine by her. She'd greet Richard, settle him in the parlor with a tot of brandy or a cup of tea before changing for dinner. Mayhap he could recommend a few acceptable ladies for Nic's consideration, some a mite less pretentious than those in her parents' social circles.

Permitting a jubilant, relieved laugh, she whirled in a circle. Finally, her betrothal would become official, and in a short while, she'd be Mrs. Major Richard Domont. Sweeping around the corridor's corner, she nearly plowed nose-first into a dark claret-covered chest.

Not Richard. The duke. Nic.

His manly scent wafted past, and she stifled the impulse to step nearer and sniff.

How could one be simultaneously so disappointed and excited?

"Easy, lass, what's your hurry?" Momentarily grasping her upper arms to steady her, Nic cocked his head and winked. "Eager to see me?"

"No. Er. Yes. That is, I am pleased to see you, Your Grace."

Nic and Osborne, the butler, exchanged an amused glance.

"I thought you were Major Domont." Katrina disentangled herself, refusing to acknowledge her breathless tone or the giddy pulse turning flip-flops behind her ribs.

Beyond Nic, the entry stood empty, the heavy door firmly closed.

Shouldn't she be horridly frustrated? Perhaps pout or shed a tear or two?

And have Nic believe her one of the ninnies she'd determined to protect him from?

Nic's eyes shadowed briefly before his jovial gaze lit once more. "No, I'm afraid you'll have to settle for me. I'm confident your major will arrive soon. I'm quite anticipating making his acquaintance."

How kind of Nic to reassure her.

Beside Nic, Osborne notched a regal brow upward. "Shall I escort his grace to the drawing room, miss?"

"I'll do it, but please notify Mama and Papa of his arrival. A tea tray would be most appreciated as well." She touched Nic's arm. "Unless you'd prefer something a big stronger?"

"Tea will suffice until after supper," Nic said, taking in the grandeur surrounding him.

Hmm, didn't he imbibe heavily? All sailors did, didn't they? There appeared much about The Saint she didn't know. Didn't think his doting aunt knew either. "Just tea and a light repast, please, Osborne."

"I shall see to it at once, miss." After angling his head deferentially, Osborne trod the corridor ahead of them.

Conscious of her ink-stained fingertips, rather than

hide them, Katrina lifted her hands and wiggled her fingers. "I've discolored fingers, Your Grace, but confess, other than a short list of desirable traits for your duchess, I've been woefully unsuccessful in compiling potential candidates' names."

"Well, one is all I require." Nic clasped his hands behind him. "I am confident you will find me a most compatible woman."

"I shall certainly try."

He fell into step beside her, their strides well-matched. "Thank you for suggesting Doctor Cutter. He said Aunt Bertie's not eating enough, particularly red meats, and not getting enough exercise either. She's not that old, just eight-and-fifty, but a life besieged by grief and anxiety ages a person."

"I'm sure it does. We've invited her to attend functions and dine with us several times, but she always refuses, saying the carriage ride would exhaust her." More likely Miss Sweeting worried about Society's reception as well as had nothing to wear. Katrina opened the drawing room's doors then stepped aside. "I assume she'll reside with you after your marriage?"

"That is my intent, though I expect she'll argue." With the ease of a man accustomed to being in command and knowing his surroundings, he entered the room and swiftly scrutinized the interior. No doubt his life had depended upon his acuteness more than once.

His attention hovered on Katrina's newly completed portrait nestled between floor-to-ceiling windows. In the painting, she wore the blue and white gown she intended to wear for her betrothal announcement.

"You cut your hair, Nic." Trailing him, she slowed her steps. "I suppose it was necessary."

Gads, she sounded positively wistful, but his hair had been extraordinarily beautiful.

He shot her an unreadable sideways look and fanned his fingers over his nape. "Aye, my solicitor advised me to. More respectable and all that. My hair hasn't been this short since I was a lad." His eyes twinkled as he rubbed his bare neck. "It kept my ears warm, and I confess to feeling rather naked. I keep jerking my head to toss my hair off my face. I suppose I look rather idiotic."

"It's much darker, more of a burnished honey now

rather than golden." Which was why she'd mistaken him for Richard.

Where was Richard?

Why hadn't he written?

Uneasiness plummeted her stomach. Enough. Fretting wouldn't produce him. She tilted her head. "I trust your trip to London proved successful?"

Tugging his earlobe, Nic nodded slowly. "Aye, though contesting the guardianship of my sisters may take a month or two."

"I imagine matters of that nature cannot be rushed." What would his sisters do in the meanwhile?

"True, but it gives me additional time to seek my bride. I promoted my first mate to captain and bade my crew a temporary farewell. *The Weeping Siren* sailed for Tortuga with the tide this morning. I saw my sisters too. They weren't exactly enthusiastic, but neither were they hostile. More than anything right now they are grieving and scared."

"This situation is profoundly difficult for you all." Uncertain why—Richard's continued absence or empathy for Nic's sisters—she swallowed against a surge of emotion tightening her throat. "I truly wish we were acquainted with Lady ... Miss—" Katrina faltered. What was she to call Nic's sisters? Never mind. They could discuss that particular later. "If we were, we could invite them to winter with us."

Nic sighed, his mossy gaze bleak and weary. "What happens if they refuse to accept me, Katrina? Cannot accept the change in their circumstances? Because of our sire's duplicity, they've gone from coddled darlings to by-blows, and even at their tender ages, they understand full well what that means. They aren't even ladies anymore, but the Misses Trehmain. He stripped them of everything, and I cannot help but think they must resent me, and rightfully so."

Katrina marched across the plush carpet, her sage skirts swooshing softly. She took his hand, though most improper, and gave it a reassuring squeeze. "A child shouldn't be blamed for his or her parents' failings. You will love your sisters and affirm them and win them over in time. And we *will* find you a wife who will accept and nurture Daphne and Delilah. And trust me, a substantial purse opens many, many doors."

She jutted her chin up a notch. "Papa is a bastard too, and few *haut ton* members dare snub or cut him. He owns most of them in one way or another, yet he's never abused his position."

Tenderness filled Nic's lovely eyes, and he traced his thumb over her lower lip before caressing her cheek. "How did one so young become so wise?"

Rustling at the doorway drew their attention, and Papa strode in.

"Pendergast, pray tell, why are you holding my daughter's hand?"

5

Nic promptly tried extracting his hand from Katrina's petal-soft palm, but she retained a firm hold. God's bones, if Needham had seen him caress her face ... An enraged father calling him out would muck up his plans entirely and set his sisters' futures tumbling pell-mell straight to Hades. He tugged and whispered, "Miss Needham—"

"Don't be silly, Papa. *I'm* holding his grace's hand." *Aye, that made all the bloody difference.* "And for a very good reason. I'm sure you'd approve."

Hardly.

Unless betrothed, unmarried, ungloved ladies of quality did not clasp a gentleman's hand for any reason. Surely she must be aware of the impropriety. Even

Nic knew that tidbit.

"I assure you, Needham, I am not holding your daughter's hand." Not precisely.

Needham's dancing eyebrows and pointed gaze alleged otherwise.

Nic wiggled his fingers, and Katrina smiled into his face, giving his hand another squeeze, as if it were the most natural thing in the world to stand before her father clasping a man's hand. A stranger's hand, at that.

Nic gave another tentative pull. Nothing except tingling fingertips.

Christ, an alligator's jaw had a weaker grasp.

"I'm comforting him," Katrina said without compunction.

I'm dead.

Bloody maggoty hell. A groan threatened, but Nic marshalled the involuntary noise. Only an innocent would admit to comforting a man and not comprehend her words' significance. Ladies most certainly didn't comfort gentleman acquaintances. Katrina's naïveté, though charming, might land him on the field of honor.

She dimpled and angled her father a guileless

glance. "He frets for his sisters, and I've promised to help him find a bride. It's all entirely innocent, I assure you."

The minx had the audacity to lift Nic's entrapped hand, which he purposed to keep relaxed, rather like a dead octopus.

Lord, but she must lead her parents a merry chase. She'd lead her husband a merry chase too, and God above, despite the impossibility, he wanted to be that damned lucky bastard.

Mr. Needham chuckled and smoothed one side of his sandy mustache. "So I see from the beleaguered looks the duke keeps sliding me. Release the poor chap else he flees before dinner, and I have to explain to your mother why the table is a guest short."

After a final reassuring, finger-numbing pulse, she rushed to her father and kissed both his cheeks. "Have you heard from Major Domont?" she murmured softly.

"Not yet, my dear." Needham patted her shoulder, his gaze compassionate. "Be patient. He'll return as promised. He adores you."

"Of course he does. How could he not?" An attractive brunette swept into the room, fairly beaming. "Don't fret about the major. The army doesn't keep to our schedules. He'll be along, darling."

Greatly resembling Katrina, except for her violet eyes, Mrs. Needham dipped a graceful curtsy. "Your Grace. I cannot tell you how delighted I am to learn of your good fortune, albeit it doesn't portend well for your unfortunate sisters."

Nic bowed. "It is an honor to see you again, Mrs. Needham."

Once the greetings had been exchanged, Katrina strayed to peek out the window. Her shoulders slumped the slightest bit, and irritation toward a man he'd never met welled within Nic. True, the major's military duties might have delayed him, but it only took a moment to jot a missive and send it off to the woman you'd professed to love and promised to marry.

If Katrina waited for *him*, he'd not dally, but return at the first opportunity. Hell, he'd never leave her.

Ever? Not even to take to the sea again?

A mule's kick to his ribs wouldn't have cramped his lungs more, and his breathing stuttered. No, that commitment he couldn't make. He loved the sea, and she wasn't a mistress who took kindly to sharing her men. If he closed his eyes and held perfectly still, he could feel her seductive rolling and swaying beneath his feet.

Nonetheless, he'd been damned disappointed to learn Katrina was practically betrothed. She'd quite captivated him in his short visit with Aunt Bertie. Nic hadn't minded her delicate hand wrapped in his the least and admitted he'd contemplated kissing her before her father barged in.

Good thing Needham had interrupted.

Nic needed her assistance—and her mother's too, of course—and he'd be a sailless, rudderless ship if they refused to further his cause because he'd foolishly overstepped the bounds. Even dukes couldn't always have what they wanted.

"Please forgive our daughter for her forwardness, Your Grace." Sending Katrina a doting glance, Mrs. Needham indicated he should have a seat on the settee beside her. "She possesses a tender heart and at times, forgets herself and what's acceptable."

Katrina's gaze meshed with his, and she cocked a shoulder. "I do. I try to remember all the rules, but when I get excited, they rush out of my head faster than water over a fall."

"It's of no import." Nic rather hated rules too, and now he must adhere to an entire litany of the wretched things. He sat, and his attention again gravitated to the portrait dominating the tastefully decorated room.

Katrina's clear blue eyes, containing the perfect blend of merriment and innocence, sparkled from the canvas. Her skin glowed like the marble statues he'd seen in Rome, and her lips perfectly matched the pink peonies she held—wherever had they acquired the blooms this time of year? A rich shade between pecan and sable, her glossy hair had been twisted into an intricate Grecian style, intertwined with pearls. More pearls as well as sapphires adorned her ears, throat, and the wrist of the hand clutching the peony bouquet. The jewels enhanced her eyes and the exquisite blue and white gown she wore.

A gown which revealed tempting cleavage.

Look away.

"The likeness is superb," Nic muttered at last, praying no one noticed his husky tone.

"It is indeed." Needham's perceptive gaze swung between his daughter's portrait and Nic several times.

Astute man. Had he heard and discerned Nic's interest?

Perhaps Needham would consider a duke rather than a major? No, a doting papa, he'd let Katrina make the choice, and she'd already picked her dashing soldier.

And Nic had chosen the sea.

"Mama, I confess, I'm having a deucedly difficult time contriving a list of seemly candidates for his grace's bride." Sinking into the chair opposite Nic, Katrina arranged her skirts and gave her mother an engaging smile. "Might I impose upon you to assist me?"

Osborne entered with the tea tray, and a few moments passed as Mrs. Needham poured tea and everyone selected a scrumptious pastry. At last, she answered her daughter.

"I should be happy to lend you my advice. I'm sure if we put our heads together, we'll muster a few acceptable ladies." She lifted the plate of assorted confections, offering Nic another, which he gratefully accepted. No flaky delicacies like this on *The Weeping Siren*.

"How fare your sisters, Pendergast?" she inquired, returning the plate to the table. "I met the dears once, several years ago. Delightful and charming, and both quite bashful."

His mouth full, Nic gulped the half-chewed Shrewsbury tart, damn near strangling in the process. He swallowed twice more, cleared his throat, took a hefty sip of tea and scalded his blasted tongue before he could speak.

Uncouth bumpkin.

"Aye, they are timid, and they've been isolated for months with a crusty barnacle of a governess as the duchess and my brother toured the continent. If I had female relatives, besides Aunt Bertie, that is, I'd promptly move my sisters in with them until I marry. I'm afraid right now, they'd be uncomfortable with only me about. I am a stranger to them, after all."

"Too bad Miss Sweeting doesn't have a bigger

house. Your sisters could live with her for the time being. She'd adore it, for she's quite lonely." Katrina sipped her tea, a far-off expression on her face.

At least she hadn't noticed him nearly choking to death or ogling her portrait.

Mrs. Needham set her china cup upon the oval tea table. "Hugo, what say you we invite Miss Sweeting and his grace's sisters to stay with us until he marries?" She flicked her fingers ceilingward. "We've several empty bedchambers, and since I presume Miss Sweeting will live with Pendergast too, it will give the ladies a chance to become acquainted before he weds."

"Surely that would be an enormous imposition," Nic demurred, though the notion appealed a great deal. Traveling between Chamberdall Court, Aunt Bertie's, London, and his appointments with Katrina wouldn't leave him much time for assemblies or courtship.

Katrina nodded eagerly, the shiny, loose curls near her ears pirouetting. "That's a splendid idea. And, since Mama and I shall work closely with his grace on finding a bride as well as helping him with a few other areas he has expressed an interest in polishing—"

She swung him an expectant look, and Nic produced a bashful grin.

"Dancing, properly knotting a cravat, which fork or spoon to use, a new wardrobe ... I'm sadly lacking in refinement," he admitted.

Needham leaned into his ornate chair, his tall frame almost too big for the dainty structure. Hands folded across his trim waist while clearly taking Nic's measure, he wiggled his fingertip.

Would Nic pass muster?

"I have no objection, and as someone born on the wrong side of the blanket myself, I can empathize with what you've endured these many years, Pendergast. Also with what your sisters will bear." He scratched his nose and hooked an ankle over his knee. "That's why I extended you the funds to buy your ship, you know, though you were hardly more than a boy. I saw your potential, your determination, and might I say, you've not disappointed."

Such a rush of emotion engulfed Nic, he couldn't find his tongue for a moment. "Thank you, sir. I cannot tell you how honored I am at your faith in me. And thank you for your generous offer to invite my sisters and aunt to stay here. I gratefully accept on their behalf."

"Wonderful." Katrina beamed as she took a dainty nibble of her biscuit.

Aunt Bertie would have a conniption at first, but she'd come round. She cherished the Needham women, and they'd encourage her to eat and exercise properly too.

A commotion at the drawing room's entrance preceded two young men around Nic's age, a plumpish, dark-haired girl, perhaps a year or two younger than Katrina, and a very fat pug.

Introductions were made to Katrina's brothers, Simon, seven-and-twenty, and Theodore, four-and-twenty, as well as Shona Atterberry, the Needham' permanent houseguest. A flat-faced, snarfing, fur-covered sausage with four legs that Katrina introduced as Sir Pugsley—Sir Pudge was more apt—begged treats from all present. A swift half an hour passed, filled with comfortable conversations, good-natured bantering, and usually two or three people talking at once.

Wonderful chaos.

A close-knit family, the Needhams' warm interactions sparked an envious craving in Nic. Except for a handful of bristly sailing chums and Aunt Bertie, he wasn't particularly close to anyone. He'd never experienced the familial intimacy the Needhams took for granted—honestly hadn't realized he'd missed it. Until now.

Needham slapped his knees before standing. "I've correspondence I must see to before dinner. Pendergast, no sense leaving only to return in a short while."

"Yes, Hugo is right, Your Grace." Mrs. Needham rose and swept her arm in an arc. "Do stay and make yourself comfortable. Read, nap ... pen a letter. Osbourne can provide you with anything you might need. Katrina, may I impose upon you to help me bundle the remaining clothing for the unfortunates? I promised Mrs. Huntington I'd have them for her tonight when she and the vicar come to dinner."

"Of course." Katrina curtsied prettily, bestowing

one of her ever-ready smiles upon him. "Until later, Your Grace."

Nic bowed, murmuring, "I look forward to dinner."

Hopefully, he could manage the meal without a repeat of the tart episode or another maladroit incident.

After the Needhams departed, Nic stared out the window. What warped providence had landed him in this household with the one woman he wanted, but couldn't have, for his duchess? He dragged a hand through his hair. Or lack of hair. That would take getting used to.

He snorted, startling Sir Pugsley from his slumber.

Nic had a whole buggered new life to get used to.

Osborne entered and, as he cleared the tea's remnants, said, "Sir, might I suggest you partake in a rest in a guest chamber before refreshing yourself and joining the others for dinner?"

"Yes, Osborne, you might, and I shall gratefully accept your offer."

Decent of the majordomo not to also suggest Nic change into something more appropriate for a dinner party. He brushed the front of his less-than-fashionable jacket. This coat was the nicest he owned, and compared to the Needhams' fancy togs, he looked to have stepped from the poor house. The cast-off clothing Katrina and her mother even now wrapped for the unfortunates were likely finer garments.

Almost two hours later, Nic stood before the grand, carved mahogany fireplace in the same drawing room, sipping a glass of superior brandy. The flames illuminated the umber liquid, much finer than the swill he regularly drank aboard ship, or in port, for that matter. He didn't frequent lofty establishments, but the same hellholes his crew favored.

Except when it came to his women and rogering.

Chattering and laughter announced the other guests' arrival several minutes ago, and they'd been ushered to the floral salon, which was probably where he was supposed to go too, and which explained why the drawing room was empty when he'd entered.

Nothing like complete social ineptness.

Still, rather than join them, he'd helped himself to a tot of brandy and, savoring the fireplace's warmth, unabashedly goggled Katrina's portrait across the room. He'd not bedded a woman in a goodly while as the slight swell in his pantaloons confirmed.

Nic had always been fastidious about swiving, to the point that his crew taunted and heckled him about his pernicketiness. His surname partially contributed to his *nom de plume,* The Saint, but his sexual selectiveness and abstinence had truly earned him the moniker. Not that he hadn't ventured into carnal delights, but he restricted his pleasure to a very few, select, disease-free women, and he always used an English overcoat. He'd beget no by-blows and have his child grow up fatherless.

Taking a healthy sip of the brandy, he savored the slow burn as it slid down his throat. Damned good stuff. This ducal business might well turn him into a dandified fribble. Rotating his neck to ease the stiff muscles caused by sleeping on a lumpy mattress two nights in a row, he sighed before wandering to stand before Katrina's portrait again.

Truly a vision. If only Fate had allowed him to meet her a few months ago, before she'd met Domont.

Of all women, she might have tempted him to leave privateering behind.

Sighing again, he tucked his chin to his chest and rubbed his sore nape.

His worn boots contrasted glaringly with the immaculate Aubusson carpet. He raised one scuffed toe, squinting at his pantaloons. An inch-long tear in the seam disappeared into his boot top. Bloody damned perfect. Best ask Needham to recommend a reputable tailor. A bootmaker and glover too. He'd rather be keelhauled than stand for hours being fitted, but he'd suffer through the measuring and pinning for Daphne and Delilah.

"You look woefully melancholy, Nic."

Nic lifted his head as Katrina, wearing virginal white with lavender ribbons, over-lace, and beading, floated across the carpet to stand before him. The charming gown's purple hues turned her eyes light periwinkle, matching the gemstones at her throat and glittering on her ears.

"You are exquisite, Katrina, a joyful sight to brighten this dreary tar's ruminations."

She dimpled prettily, and holding her skirts wide, whirled around once. "Isn't it unbelievable what a lovely gown, a few jewels, and a talented abigail can do? I feel like the princess I pretended to be as a little girl."

She took no credit for her loveliness? Could she really be so unassuming and modest? She'd led a pampered life, yet demonstrated none of the characteristics of an indulged and pampered society miss.

"What were you thinking just now? You seemed much too serious." She touched his arm but, considering the wide open doors, must have thought better of it and let her hand drop to her side.

"Actually, I was contemplating the horror of having to acquire a new wardrobe." He winked, and lowered his head conspiratorially. "I quite hate fittings."

Rising on her lavender-slippered toes, she grasped his shoulder and whispered in his ear, "I do too."

Arousal surged, immediate and primal.

If he rotated his head, a mere two inches, his mouth would brush hers. What would she do if he took the liberty? Slap him? Screech? Rant? Or would betrayed accusation fill her beautiful, trusting eyes?

He couldn't bear to hurt Katrina, so he kicked his ardor to the room's farthest corner and commanded it to stay there.

"Major Domont won't be here for dinner. To Mama's chagrin, the table will be uneven after all."

To Katrina's chagrin as well.

Settling her heels on the lushly carpeted floor once more, she sliced a sideways glance at the now-closed curtains. Though she valiantly hid her hurt, he recognized pain in her hushed tone, saw confusion in the less-than-vibrant gaze she turned on him.

"I'm sure he has a valid reason." Not unless he'd been abducted by highwaymen, pressed into service aboard a ship, or died, the mangy cur.

"Yes, I suppose." She conjured a cheerful smile. "Let's start your lessons tonight, shall we?"

So like her to put aside her worries and focus on someone else's needs. Few people possessed such unselfishness, and even fewer within her social set.

"I've asked that you be seated beside me, Nic. Observe what I do, and you will be fine."

She placed her hand on his arm, and lust sluiced to every pore. God help him. He was in bloody damned trouble when it came to her. Only an idiot would subject himself to her company day after day when he'd already fallen hard despite knowing full well she could never be his.

Katrina's sweet perfume wafted upward, and Nic's groin pulsed. He needed a woman, moaning her pleasure beneath him. It had been months since he'd found release. That was why he responded to her like a rutting stag.

Ballocks.

"Everyone else has already left for the dining room. I asked Mama if I might wait and accompany you, since, when you didn't join us in the salon, I suspected you might be slightly uncomfortable."

"Your consideration is touching, but I'm not suffering from discomfort as much as ineptitude. I failed to inquire where I should meet my host and hostess, and then succumbed to your father's excellent brandy." As he set his empty tumbler aside, he winked to lighten her mood. What a pair they were, both in the doldrums this evening. "I vow, I'll commit a social *faux pas*. Use the wrong fork, speak to a guest about a taboo subject, gulp rather than sip my wine, talk with my mouth full ..."

She shook her silky head, the candles catching the coppery highlights. "Nic, you'll be fine. It's just my family, Miss Atterberry, and a few other guests, none of whom outrank you."

Outside the dining room's entrance, she hesitated. Conversation, occasional laughter, and the clatter of crystal, silver, and dishes carried into the corridor.

"Do be mindful of that stunning blond sitting next to Simon. She's Phoebe Belamont, a title-hungry termagant. She'd treat your sisters horridly. The woman wearing the garish turban is her aunt. A pushy fussock, so if you value your virtue, watch yourself. They'd trap you into marriage faster than a frog gobbles a fly."

His virtue?

He nearly laughed aloud at Katrina's concern for his honor. She took her ducal-wife- hunting duties seriously, precious darling.

Leaning nearer, he inhaled her perfume again, enjoying the satiny skin exposed by her gown's low bodice, even if the swells tantalized him unmercifully. "Why did your mother invite them if they're so objectionable?"

Katrina tightened her hand upon his arm, and Nic stole another glance at the Belamonts.

"Mama didn't. Wouldn't either. Ever. They're horrid," she whispered, "and I cannot abide them. No one can." Her nostrils flared, pink dotted her high cheeks, and her stiff shoulders, tense brows, as well as the hand clamping his forearm further revealed her distress. "You wait, Phoebe will say something nasty to me, and I'll have to be polite and pretend I don't know what she means."

"Why are they here then?" Another societal dictate—forced to endure the presence of people one couldn't stomach. As a privateer, he'd been spared the ridiculousness and surrounded himself with people whose company he enjoyed.

"They came on the Huntingtons' coat sleeves, unannounced, as always. Osborne was quite put out, as was Cook. They had to scramble to accommodate two more guests." She bent forward a mite and pointed to a cleric. "The Huntingtons are the kindly rector and his wife, and somehow the Belamonts are related. They visit quite often, usually arriving unexpectedly and staying past their welcome. By the time they depart, Mrs. Huntington is nipping the communion wine."

Nic couldn't contain his low chuckle.

"I wasn't aware they'd returned since they were here a mere fortnight ago, or I'd never have invited you to dinner and subjected you to their company." Katrina's abundant lashes swept closed, and she inhaled a bracing breath. She opened her eyes a moment later. "The final couple is Lord and Lady Gervais."

As they entered the noisy room, Miss Belamont boldly met Nic's gaze. Seductively arching, thrusting her full breasts upward, and half-closing her peridot-green eyes, she resembled a great indulged Persian cat. No innocent miss there, by George.

"Why, Miss Needham. Wherever is your handsome Major Domont?" Miss Belamont cooed, her pale green eyes wide and innocent while pointedly peering at the empty entrance before snagging on Nic's groin.

Avast, there's the predicted snide inquiry.

Katrina stiffened and lifted her pert nose fractionally, but didn't answer. No, she definitely didn't favor Miss Belamont.

Neither did he, if he'd read Miss Belamont correctly in the few moments he'd assessed her. Beautiful, spoiled, full of her own importance, and a bully, hiding her malice behind politely worded, barbed questions and feigned concern.

"Curse me for a lubber. A veritable shark. I shall heed your warning," Nic whispered as he pushed in Katrina's chair, grateful Miss Belamont and her generously exposed bosom sat across and near the table's head, while his assigned seat put him safely at the foot.

A pout upon her painted lips, the gilflurt cut Nic a ravenous, sidelong look and not-so-casually brushed a hand across her bosom.

The chit was nothing but a prettily packaged trull.

Aye, he saw Miss Belamont's breasts gushing over her scarlet bodice. He also observed the other guests' discomfort with her provocative exhibition evidenced in the vexed lines furrowing their foreheads and tense brackets framing their mouths. By God, if she shifted abruptly, her bubbies would pop loose of their straining confines and plop into her soup.

"Wasn't he to have returned by now?" Miss Belamont breathed a heavy, decidedly unsympathetic *tsk*.

Her spiteful titter met with flat stares from those assembled and a glower from the younger Needham brother. Two four-stemmed silver candelabras' glow lent a delicate radiance to Katrina's composed countenance, enhancing her ivory skin as the air fairly sparked with charged tension.

Miss Belamont's brows winged upward in artificial distress, and she splayed her hand across her chest again.

That game already grew tiresome.

Mrs. Huntington, her lips pursed in displeasure, rolled her eyes while Mrs. Needham darted Katrina a sympathetic glance.

Nic clamped his teeth and, for Katrina's sake, forced himself to remember his ragged manners and abstained from telling the Belamont chit to shut her goddamned yawp and cover her teats. However, his rigid jaw didn't stop the stream of salty oaths directed at her that paraded through his head. Pity his ducal role didn't permit him the same freedoms a privateer enjoyed, or he would've laid a verbal lashing on Miss Belamont the twopenny wench would not soon forget.

"Oh dear, never say you've had a lover's spat?" Would Miss Belamont never leave off harping? "Should we assume the expected betrothal announcement won't be forthcoming?

The shrew needed her tongue pruned.

As she'd no doubt intended, every eye focused on Katrina, although, with the exception of Miss Belamont's corpulent aunt greedily slurping her soup, concern or compassion colored their gazes.

With poised deliberation, Katrina unfolded her serviette and, after draping the cloth across her lap, regally lifted her head and calmly met the other woman's probing stare. "Nothing of the sort. Major Domont's been detained in Cambridge on army business."

Miss Belamont's lips edged upward in feline satisfaction.

Damn my blood.

A shrieking alarm pealed in Nic's brain, the same warning that had saved his life on more than one occasion. Miss Belamont meant to draw blood. Katrina's blood.

Katrina tilted her head at an endearing angle, refusing to cow to the hellcat.

Bravo, plucky darling.

He slipped his hand beneath the table and found her icy fingers. She responded with her alligator clamp, and he welcomed the numbing vice. It showed her strength even amidst her trepidation.

"Cambridge? Are you quite certain?" Miss Belamont dipped her spoon into the cream of asparagus soup, her smile brittle. "Aunt Miriam, didn't we see Major Domont in Stratford-Upon-Avon last week?"

Katrina's grip tightened, and Nic hid a wince. Hell's bells. Who knew a woman could have such strong hands?

"Oh, yes, we did indeed." Mrs. Belamont took a noisy sip of soup before looking 'round the table at everyone's stunned or distressed expressions. "He had a young lady on his arm. A very pregnant young lady."

6

Katrina managed to drag a shallow expanse of air into her lungs. And then another slightly bigger breath. Though only due to Nic's reassuring hand clasping hers and his thumb trailing back and forth across her knuckles, calming her fitful pulse and even more juddery thoughts. Scandalous and ruinous if anyone caught them holding hands beneath the lattice-patterned tablecloth.

Propriety be hanged.

She squeezed his fingers and rejoiced in the immediate counter-pulse. Stunned from the verbal pummeling she'd just endured, Katrina required the strength he lent. Springing from her chair and bolting from the room, though tempting, would give Phoebe

Belamont a satisfaction Katrina would never permit. And tearing the burgundy ribbons from Phoebe's perfectly coiffed curls, though immensely gratifying, would shame Katrina's parents.

Was Richard in Stratford-Upon-Avon?

No, no, the Belamonts must be mistaken.

She'd not jump to hasty, emotional conclusions without evidence.

They'd seen him.

Perhaps they'd only *thought* the man was Richard.

"Men oft' look similar in uniforms," Simon said, leveling Miss Belamont a cold stare.

"Yes, indeed," Shona piped in, nodding enthusiastically while marshalling a how-could-you? scowl for Phoebe. Fork in hand, Shona looked ready to stab her across the table. "That might very well be the case. Why, half the time, I cannot tell one officer from another unless I stand directly before him."

Precious, loyal dear.

"Surely a plausible explanation exists if, indeed, the Belamonts are correct." Patting his mouth with his serviette, Nic murmured the comment for Katrina's ears alone, and she gave a jerky nod.

So Richard had absentmindedly named the wrong township?

Unlikely as snow in July. Pink snow.

Stop.

Richard hadn't lied to her before. Had he? His many absences—a week or two at a time ... Not uncommon for an officer, but a faultless defense against a woman's qualms and suspicions.

"Trust him." Another whispered encouragement from Nic amidst the stilted conversations the others attempted in order to cover the dreadful awkwardness.

The diners could no more have ignored the Belamonts' insinuations than they could've a singing, dancing goat upon the table. Bless Nic for trying. Once more, he sought to reassure Katrina, this man she'd known but three days.

She had trusted Richard. Until now. She loathed the suspicion tangling her thoughts, cramping her lungs, barraging her middle with jagged-bladed knives.

Swallowing hard, her mouth gone dry as summer grass and her voice sure to crack if she spoke, Katrina summoned every ounce of pluck she possessed and, with a steady hand and nonchalant glance at Papa, casually took a sip of wine.

True, humiliation beleaguered her, by Miss Belamont's calculated design, but without evidence, Katrina refused to convict Richard. Appearances weren't always what they seemed, and besides, they weren't actually betrothed. He owed her nothing except, perhaps, an explanation.

Not entirely accurate.

Richard had asked her to marry him, had promised he'd ask Papa for her hand, had begged her to be patient while he put his affairs in order. Mayhap *she*, the unnamed woman, was the affair he'd needed to order? If Richard were involved with another woman—*God help me bear the shame*—one in the family way ... that explained his reluctance, the litany of excuses, and the continual delays.

Have I been a gullible dunderhead, refusing to see what's been before me all this while?

"Major Domont has three sisters, Miss Belamont, as well as several female cousins." Mama's eyes spewed violet sparks, and from her hand's reflexive balling atop the table, she longed to slap the superior expression from the beauty's face, though her modulated tone revealed none of her contempt. "And his familial home is near Stratford-Upon-Avon as well. There are any number of reasons he might have been there with an enceinte woman upon his arm, if it was even the major whom you saw."

How had Mama known those interesting snippets when Katrina had been ignorant of them? Richard refused to speak of his family, claiming an estrangement. She'd ask that exact question the second she caught her mother alone. But, by Hades, she'd gnaw harness leather before allowing Phoebe Belamont to see her disconcerted.

"Oh, it most certainly was him, and he wasn't in uniform either." Miss Belamont fairly preened under the attention, her wide-eyed gaze vacillating between Nic and Katrina. "I spoke with the major myself, though he did seem in a terrible rush. Barely civil to Aunt Miriam and me, he was, and the woman with him spoke not a word. Why—"

114

Papa loudly cleared his throat. "I've always held the opinion that it's unjust to discuss a person unless they are present to give an account themselves. Some might call talking behind a person's back tattlemongering or gossiping." A censuring brow raised, the last words he directed straight at a flushing Miss Belamont.

She huffed unbecomingly and flounced in her chair, her arms folded, which launched her bosoms frightfully higher.

On either side of her, Simone's and Vicar Huntington's studious absorption in their cooling soup conveyed their awareness of her indecorous display and their commendable effort to ignore the bouncing mounds.

"Tell me, Huntington," Papa said, "was that a new pair of bays I saw before your landau today? Beautiful steppers, I must say." He neatly quashed any further mention of Richard as the men launched into an impromptu horseflesh discussion, floundering and blathering like half-drowned men seizing a single lifeline.

Would that Katrina's riotous musings could so easily be quelled. Her stomach twisted and knotted sickeningly, but she had promised to help Nic tonight. She selected a soup spoon and casually dipped its side into the bowl, taking care to skim from the front to the back.

Nic immediately mimicked her.

Miss Belamont's narrowed gaze and petulant pout conveyed her displeasure, but for the rest of the meal, she conducted herself with unexpected restraint.

Over an hour later, Mama and Papa having wisely foregone the gentlemen's customary post-dinner libation, all the diners assembled in the drawing room. Nic chatted with Papa and Mr. Huntington, but every now and again, sent her a heartening look. His haircut lent him a refined air, but his carriage and mannerisms clearly bespoke a man of humbler—no, not humbler … unpretentious—origins. And she admired that. It set him apart from the *ton*'s fops and dandies, whom she'd never found appealing.

Mama and Shona flanked her on the settee, not a coincidence to be sure, as Mrs. Huntington settled onto the pianoforte's smallish bench and proceeded to play one soothing tune after another.

The rest of the evening passed pleasantly enough, though everyone dutifully abstained from mentioning Richard again. A headache thrummed behind Katrina's eyes, and though she'd intended to engage Nic in a wife-hunting conversation, she, instead, yielded to her need to be alone. Impossible to sort through her topsy-turvy thoughts with so many people about. Besides, if she had to watch Phoebe Belamont gushing over Nic any longer, what little dinner Katrina had gagged down would make a violent reappearance.

Katrina gave Mama's hand a pat. "Please forgive me, but I fear I've developed a fierce headache and should like to retire early."

"I don't wonder," Shona commiserated. She leaned near, giving Katrina a sisterly hug and whispering in her ear, "You've performed marvelously. That she-cat is practically hissing and scratching in frustration."

Looked more like purring in lust to Katrina.

"Of course, my pet." Mama bussed Katrina's cheek, saying quietly, "Go along then. Be sure to arrange what time his grace will call tomorrow for his comportment lessons."

Shona giggled and slid him a covert peek. "Poor man. To be his age and have to suffer through that balderdash. I pity him."

Katrina's attention involuntarily strayed to Nic again, as it had repeatedly throughout the evening. Finding Miss Belamont clinging to his arm snugger than a barnacle embedded on a whale grated.

"He's not completely without social graces," Katrina said. "A little polishing, and he'll be quite presentable. I can think of more than one peer whose manners are impeccable, but who is nevertheless a boorish lout. Manners do not a gentleman make."

I rather like Nic as he is.

She did prefer the rough privateer, and she oughtn't to favor him at all. She should be beside herself with angst that her intended had, perhaps, thrown her over, or at the very least, not been forthright.

Pregnant woman— No. Not now.

She stood, and the movement drew Nic's attention.

With practiced finesse, he extracted his arm from Miss Belamont's clinging grasp. With five long paces, he reached Katrina's side. "Mrs. Needham, might I have a word with you and Miss Needham? Perhaps we could step into the corridor?"

Katrina checked a smile. One didn't conduct conversations in the passageways. "I think the library would suit better."

After Mama rose, she clasped his extended elbow and nodded to her other guests. "Please excuse us. His grace requires a moment with Katrina and me."

As she swept from the drawing room, Katrina did smile, broadly and a touch gloatingly, at Phoebe Belamont.

Once in the library, Katrina lit a pair of tapers in the dual holder atop her writing desk. No fire burned in the grate, and the muted candlelight only illuminated a small sphere.

Nic faced them, and a hint of uncertainty hovered around his daunting form. "When would be most convenient to collect my sisters and aunt? I don't wish to impose upon your hospitality until you're prepared."

He rubbed his nape. "I confess, I'm completely out of my element with all of this."

Katrina angled her head. He didn't like indebtedness, nor was he accustomed to deferring to others. His title afforded him as much—more—power in many regards than his captaincy had, yet he hesitated to wield his status. Perchance had no desire to?

What kind of captain had he been? Fair and just, Katrina gathered from his treatment of his aunt and concern for his sisters. More a comrade to his crew than a master?

Mama tutted and waved her hand before straightening a couple of volumes. "As soon as possible is perfectly fine. I'll have the servants make the beds, and I shall assign maids to assist your aunt and sisters. Unless they have their own? What about a governess? Should I have a room readied for her as well?"

"No, I've dismissed their governess. She was mean, neglectful, and I suspect had a penchant for brandy." He breathed out a controlled sigh. "That's another thing I beg your guidance for since you've a daughter." His hooded gaze trailed to Katrina. "I ha-

120

ven't the first notion what constitutes an acceptable governess."

"Yes, you do." Katrina lifted her hand and ticked off her fingers. "A respectable woman who's not given to unkindness, inattention, or tipping a flask too readily." She lifted a fourth finger. "And, from my personal experiences, a lady who doesn't have a particular preference for garlic and onions," up went her thumb, "and doesn't regularly remove her shoes and expose her charges to her malodorous feet."

Her monologue met with a rich, throaty chuckle, and Nic grinned. "I'll make a mental note, particularly of the latter."

Mama tapped her chin. "I think the girls should share a room, so they aren't lonely or frightened in their new environ." A keen glint entered her eyes. "Your Grace, where do *you* intend to reside?"

Nic clasped his hands behind him and rocked onto his heels.

Ah, the privateer again.

"I shall either stay at Aunt Bertie's or a nearby inn."

Mama shook her raven head. "No inns close by, I fear. May I propose you stay with us as well? As I said earlier, we've plenty of room, and having you about will give your sisters more opportunity to become acquainted with you in a less formal setting."

Katrina's heart tripped. Nic sleeping beneath the same roof? Eating every meal with her? Perhaps reading in the library or playing cards in the parlor?

What would Richard think?

He could think whatever he liked. If, and when, he bothered to appear. And if he never did, Nic's presence made no difference. Besides, she wasn't carrying on an illicit affair with him, for heaven's sake.

He had a young lady on his arm. A very pregnant young lady.

He did seem in a terrible rush. Barely civil to Aunt Miriam.

Blast and bother. Her ruminations brought the Belamonts' words crashing into her mind, bathing her in distress. Had Richard betrayed her? Their love? What did a person do in this circumstance? Wait and hope he had a valid reason? Send the Bow Street Runners after him? Pen a polite note inquiring if their courtship had ended? For all the *haut ton*'s rules and recommendations on decorous behavior, nothing addressed this ugliness.

Mama's consideration shifted to Katrina, and even in the dim light, something in addition to warmth tinged her mother's eyes. "And, I think having you here would do Katrina a wealth of good to divert her from this evening's unpleasant developments."

"Mama!" Good God. Must Mama bring that up now? Had she guessed Katrina's thoughts? "I promise you, I'm not about to succumb to a fit of the blue devils. I'm confident we'll know the truth of it soon enough."

She wasn't confident at all, but whining and moping served no purpose, though if Richard had thrown her over, she'd be hard-pressed to maintain her stoic front. Perhaps she could persuade her parents to take a trip abroad for several months.

Papa couldn't leave the bank that long.

Well, then her and Mama.

"If you're certain it wouldn't be an inconvenience

...?" Nic spoke to her mother, but his sharp gaze rested upon Katrina.

"Not in the least." Mama shook her head once.

He grinned and inclined his head, his dimple and scar catching the candles' meager light. "Then, I should be honored to accept your hospitality. Now if you will excuse me, I'll bid Needham and the others a good evening. I've much to do, not the least of which is to inform my aunt she'll be taking up residence here." He chuckled again, the deep baritone reverberating off the book-laden shelves. "She'll kick up a fuss, I've no doubt."

"Only for a trifling, but once she's here, I'm sure she'll be glad of it," Katrina assured him.

"Until the day after tomorrow, ladies." He kissed Mama's hand before bending over Katrina's.

Broad-shouldered and commanding, Nic strode from the room, his swagger that of a man accustomed to walking decks rather than expensive, plush carpets or marbled floors. He possessed a masculine grace, impressive and imposing.

"Are you smitten?"

Her mother's soft question yanked Katrina's focus from the empty doorway.

"Pardon?" Smitten, as in attracted to? Enamored of? Captivated by? Katrina collected her clambering thoughts. "What a peculiar question. Why would you ask such a thing?"

"I expected Miss Belamont's revelation to produce a much stronger reaction, Kitty, and I didn't miss his grace's murmuring in your ear during dinner. He calms you in a way I've never seen before."

Katrina hugged her mother for an extended moment, scrambling for an honest explanation.

"Mama, he's a friend whom I'm happy to help. In some ways, he and I are alike, both born outside Society's boundaries, yet thrust into the din because of our parents' status. You know full well there are those who still turn their haughty noses up when in our presence, and I suspect his grace will bear a fair share of snobbery despite his lofty title. Jealousy and envy are toxic, piercing weapons. Perhaps it's because we know we're safe from romantic entanglement with the other that we can relax and be ourselves, and I find it quite refreshing, truth to tell."

Even as she murmured the words, Katrina knew them only partially true. If she weren't already romantically involved, Nic was precisely the kind of man who could capture her heart.

"*Hmph*. Call it what you will, my dear." After blowing out the candles, her mother looped her hand through Katrina's arm as they left the library, their slippers swishing in unison. "But I was young once too, and the way he looks at you isn't fraternal. Perhaps I shouldn't have asked him to stay."

Surely Mama misread Nic. He looked upon her with an acquaintance's regard.

"Mama, he needs friends, and I assure you, I'm not about to fall in love with a scoundrel who'll return to the sea the moment his sisters are raised and wed." No, she'd fallen in love with a soldier whose face she'd had a deuced time recalling since a certain oversized swashbuckler with ridiculously green eyes discovered her crawling across his aunt's floor.

At the stairs, Mama cupped Katrina's face. "Dearest, I hope with all my heart Major Domont's delay is nothing more than an army matter, but you may need to prepare ..." She inhaled a lungful and released it with a whoosh. "Well, I needn't say it, my darling, need I?"

Tears glimmered in her lovely violet eyes.

"No, Mama, you needn't, but I must know for certain." Suddenly weary and fighting tears, Katrina cast her gaze to the first riser. Rejection stung. Brutally. The sooner she knew the truth, the sooner she could reevaluate her future. "Can you ask Papa to see to it for me? Send one of his men to Stratford-upon-Avon and discover why Major Domont is there? Out of uniform?"

"I'll have him do so first thing on the morrow." Laughter and music echoed from the open drawing room doors, and Mama lowered her voice, two lines creasing her worried brow. "And if it's discovered your major isn't worthy, Kitty?"

What a polite way to call Richard a philandering cockscum.

"Well, I suppose I'll need to seek elsewhere for a husband, won't I?" In a decade. Either a man she hadn't given her heart to, or one who wouldn't mash the organ beneath his polished boots.

"Yes, there's always next Season." Mama nodded, a falsely bright smile wreathing her face. "That will give you a chance to recover ... unless ... you've someone in mind already?"

Katrina lifted her skirts, and placing a foot on the lowest stair, rolled her shoulders while issuing a pathetic little laugh before quipping, "The Duke of Pendergast seeks a wife."

Eyes half-open, Nic yawned and stretched his legs before him. On the coach's opposite side, his sisters slept, tucked into each other. Shy to the point of awkwardness, Daphne and Delilah hardly spoke since he'd collected them this morning and left instructions with Chamberdall Court's housekeeper to send their trunks by wagon no later than the next day.

They adamantly refused to address him by his given name, but instead whispered, "Yes, Your Grace or No, Your Grace." Someone, likely their now-former governess, had filled their heads with twaddle that had them pale and terrified in his presence.

Aunt Bertie snored softly beside him, her black-bonneted head resting on his shoulder as Percival napped in a basket atop her lap. Amidst his sisters' muffled giggles, and Percival's yowls and hisses, Nic, Dalton, and Aunt Bertie had maneuvered the obstinate cat into the hamper. Not without a few scratches, flying fur, and several muttered oaths.

Cats—fat, pampered cats—were not meant to travel in smallish enclosures.

To his delight and surprise, Aunt Bertie proved remarkably agreeable about trotting off to the Needhams'. So much so that he found himself almost asking why several times. After all, Daphne and Delilah weren't directly related to her, so her zeal to become acquainted confounded a mite.

Before falling asleep, she'd murmured something about a grand exploit. He'd hardly call an extended visit with a former pupil and her family an adventure, but then again, he'd traveled extensively and seen more in his six-and-twenty years than most people did in a lifetime. To his aunt, venturing to the Needhams' for a few weeks might, indeed, be a splendid adventure.

Daphne shifted, and Nic's sisters captured his interest once more.

For all Collingsworth's blustering, he hadn't bothered to collect the girls and ensconce them in his London house, even five weeks after their mother's death. Probably because he already had four unmarried daughters underfoot and only cared about the guardianship's monetary provision, with which he'd no doubt padded his thin pockets.

Naming Collingsworth Daphne's and Delilah's guardian still didn't make sense when Pendergast had intended to reveal Nic's legitimacy, unless the old duke had meant it as a temporary arrangement until Nic could be notified of his inheritance.

Nic scratched his cheek, unused to the smooth-shaven skin. No telling what maggot warped his sire's reasoning, but he had a legacy of dubious decisions. Pray God the deficit wasn't hereditary.

Flexing his legs, he rested his head against the ducal carriage's plush squabs. The old duke had a bloody fine coach house filled with more conveyances than anyone possibly had need of. The same could be said of the stables. How many horses did one man require?

Or manors, for that matter? Nic's man of business had advised him that he owned seven, not including the Berkley Square residence and a townhouse in Mayfair. Not for long. He intended to sell every unentailed property and, with the funds, establish trusts for his sisters.

Daphne and Delilah would be quite wealthy in their own right, a distinct advantage with a tarnished pedigree. A derisive, and wholly gratified, grin tipped Nic's mouth. Wouldn't old Pendergast turn flips in his grave if he knew Nic's scheme?

Delilah sighed, the low sound forlorn, and in her sleep, Daphne snuggled closer, wrapping her arms around her younger sister, even as Aunt Bertie snorted and situated herself more comfortably against him.

His family.

They'd want for nothing, and more importantly, they'd know happiness again. He'd see to it. A foreign peace engulfed him, and he indulged the unfamiliar sensation for a few minutes, letting his mind wander to Katrina.

Neither she nor Mrs. Needham had heard him step

from the drawing room after saying his farewells. Unaware that he stood at the entry, they'd ascended the stairs, their heads close together and arms about each other's waists. Hopefully his wife, whoever she should be, would treat his sisters thusly.

The Duke of Pendergast seeks a wife.

Had Katrina been serious?

What rot. Of course not.

More likely, the evening's strain had her tossing the flippant remark. Not that he minded the path her mind had journeyed down. Quite the opposite, in fact. Though improbable, Nic found the notion most agreeable. Her heartache, he did not. Did he want to be the man she wed because another had rejected her?

You don't know that.

Besides, wedding Katrina wasn't an option, even if she already occupied a portion of his heart. A man didn't embark on voyages and leave a woman with her buoyant, considerate temperament for months, or even years. She'd be lonely and miserable, and perhaps, in time, grow resentful and bitter. Her kind needed her husband close, to share life's experiences with, especially if children came along.

But never to sail again, even after his *lettre de marque*'s revocation? His pulse, his breathing, pulsed in rhythm to the sea's tides. What could possibly compare to that magic?

Just as well Domont had a prior claim on Katrina, and damn his eyes, he'd better have a blasted good reason for strutting around with another woman on his arm. Nic fisted his hands. And for not having the decency to contact Katrina ... Kitty.

A curiosity-born grin tipped his lips. Soft and sweet kitten? Or playful and mischievous?

He'd soon find out, as they'd be sharing a roof—a prospect simultaneously wonderful and awful. Nic could take his fill of Katrina's presence, but coveting a woman whose heart belonged to another, and one he didn't dare entertain wishful fantasies about, would not end well for him. But none of this was about him. His sisters and his aunt must be kept at his mind's forefront.

What he did, he did for them.

And someday, when Aunt Bertie had passed and

Daphne and Delilah were happily married with children on their knees, he could say the sacrifice had been worth it. And what if he and his duchess were blessed with children? What then? Would he desert his children for the sea? Those troublesome musings he shoved to a dark corner of his mind, to examine later. Much later.

By the time they arrived at the Needhams' ostentatious manor, late afternoon had descended, with her predictable wintertime gloom and chill. In short order, his aunt and sisters were hustled inside, relieved of their outer garments, and shown to their chambers with the promise of warm baths, hot chocolate, and a light repast.

Rather than avail himself of his chamber, Nic sought the library, intent on selecting a volume or two. Having never had access to so many books, he craned his neck, gaping at the top shelves. Thousands of books beckoned, row upon row of varying sizes, surely a goodly number generations old.

Katrina slipped into the room, and he sent her a smile as he climbed a ladder to its topmost rung. "I've always wanted to do this." Holding the ladder's sides, he leaned away and grinned.

Eyes twinkling, she smiled back. "Do what?"

"Have so many books to choose from, I needed a ladder to reach the uppermost volumes."

She played with a sofa pillow's tassels, stroking the silk threads. "I'm sure Chamberdall Court has an extensive library."

Probably a mammoth one. But he was here. Now.

A gold-embossed red leather drew his eye, and Nic pulled the volume from the shelf. He inhaled the heady aroma. "What about this one?"

Katrina perched on a chair's padded arm, the pillow in her lap, and shook her shiny head, sending her pearl teardrop earbobs bouncing. "Unless you're searching for a volume on animal husbandry," she squinted at the book he held, "specifically, the reproduction of poultry, you may want to reconsider your choice."

"*Hmph*, can't say I have a need to know which came first, the chicken or the egg, right now." Or ever. Nic replaced the book and waved a careless hand.

"Don't suppose there's anything here about how to raise decorous young women?"

"Of course, but the reading is as dry as ash and utterly ridiculous." After tossing the pillow onto the sofa, she stepped to a shelf near the door. "They're located over here." She bent and ran her fingers along a row of books before selecting two thin, blue-green tomes. "*The Lady's Guide to Proper Comportment*," she raised the first book, "and *The Genteel Lady's Guide to Practical Living*. Both guaranteed to bore your sisters and you to death."

She made a dramatic pose, eyes closed and the back of her hand pressed to her forehead.

Was there a gentleman's comportment equivalent? For him? One step at a time.

"Excellent." Deftly descending the ladder, he indicated the books with a nod. "Have you read either?"

"Both, multiple times. Usually for penance after flouting a social rule." After laying the books on the smallish desk, she leaned against it and chuckled, a light, joyful burble. "I fear they failed to transform me into a wholly proper miss. I tend to disregard the parts

I think drivel, which, honestly, are most, yet I get along manageably well." She wrinkled her nose adorably. "Mama and society might not agree, but I've become quite accomplished at acting the part."

His lips twitched. Good for her.

"May I offer a word of advice, Nic?" She brushed her fingers along a quill's feather lying in its feminine porcelain holder.

"By all means." A scribbled, crossed-off paper lay upon the desktop. Was that his bride list?

"I'd give your sisters a bit of time before trying to transform them. I'm certain, as a duke's daughters, they've already had comportment drilled into them until they want to scream. Let them breathe a little, come out of the shells they've retreated into."

"Sound advice, and a recommendation I'll gratefully heed." He had no more desire to read tedious decorum instructions than his sisters likely had to hear them. Once he'd reached the floor, Nick straightened his coat. "What do you suggest then? For my reading enjoyment?"

"I rather like Chaucer's works." Speaking over her

shoulder, Katrina glided to a shorter shelf adjacent to the desk. "We have them all, and *The Canterbury Tales* might be shared with your sisters too."

In the distance, carriage wheels crunched upon gravel.

A visitor?

Major Domont or one of the Needhams returning home?

Katrina didn't even glance toward the window.

She's given up on Domont.

"Have you heard from your major?" Nic touched her shoulder. Far too bold and forward, but though she valiantly hid her doldrums behind bright smiles, ennui lingered in her troubled gaze.

Absorbed in the lace edging her gown's sleeve, Katrina gave one short shake of her head, the curls framing her face bobbing merrily. The sole part of her remotely cheery. Even her gown, a demure fawn edged in Spanish brown braiding and creamy lace, bespoke her low spirits.

"No, but Papa's sent a man to Stratford-Upon-Avon." Her lower lip clenched between her teeth, her sable lashes swept downward, concealing her desolate blue eyes and fanning her porcelain cheeks. She released an unsteady sigh. "We've no word from Peters, Papa's man, yet."

So vulnerable, yet so brave. So in need of comforting.

True, there were worse things than being thrown over, but a woman in love couldn't see beyond the pain rending her cracked heart and the mortification slashing her wounded soul.

"My sympathies." Condolences? What did one say in a situation like this?

Certainly not what he truly thought. "You're well rid of the inconsiderate bilge rat." Or "Don't waste your tears on the unmitigated arse." Or even, "Allow me the pleasure of cobbing the blackguard for his villainy."

"Thank you, I think." Katrina shrugged. "It is what it is."

Why didn't she rail or cry? Protest the injustice? Damn Domont's soul to Davy Jones's locker? Because she wasn't vindictive or vengeful. Emotion burgeoned behind his ribs, and in that instant, Nic would have willingly forsaken sailing to claim her as his.

"Perhaps he's been ill, Katrina, or—"

She held up her hand, palm facing Nic, and raised tear-glassy eyes to his, her smile tremulous and pain-riddled. "Trust me. I've thought of every possible scenario, and only a turnip-brain refuses to see what's clearly before them."

Again the urge to sweep her into his arms and soothe her worries overcame him.

And if they were caught in an embrace, then what? Ruination, dishonor, and not a marooned sailor's chance of marrying Domont if the jackanape came 'round in the end. She'd be forced to marry Nic.

Would that be so awful?

She brushed her fingertips across one brow and sighed softly. "You'll forgive me for not wishing to speak on it."

"Of course." Damn Domont's eyes. Keelhauling was too good for him. So was running the gauntlet, the scamping cur.

Putting her bent forefinger to her eye's corner,

Katrina averted her head, but not before she knuckled a tear away.

Damn the risk.

Nic gently drew her into his arms, one hand pressed to her slender waist and the other to her head resting against his chest. "I'm willing to bet you've been stoic and practical the past two days, and haven't indulged in a good cry."

"I'm not given to waterworks," she mumbled into his shirtfront. "Besides, my face becomes splotchy, and my nose reddens horridly. I resemble a squalling new-born, which, I assure you, is frightful on an adult."

Nonetheless, her throaty response revealed the tears clogging her throat.

He tipped her chin and winked. "A beautiful, squalling newborn, I'd wager."

Pleasure lit her eyes, and a flush crept over her cheeks, pinkening them.

So easily pleased. Didn't Domont compliment her?

"If you are this kind to your sisters, they'll come to worship you in no time." Her focus dropped to his mouth and remained there.

Exactly what he'd been contemplating, had been yearning to do, these past five days.

Slowly, to ease any alarm and give Katrina time to stop him, Nic bent his neck, edging his mouth nearer and nearer.

She parted her lips, her breath sweet and faintly smelling of tea and lemon.

He touched his mouth to hers, tentative, testing. Even that light, feathery touch thrilled to his soles. An electrical jolt seared his chest, spiraling outward to his limbs. Nic tightened his embrace and traced his tongue across her lips, nudging the soft pillows apart.

A delicate gasp escaped her, but she didn't yank away. Rather, she stood on her toes and crept her hands up his arms to clutch his shoulders.

An unexpected, but oh so welcome and cherished, gift.

Groaning, he availed himself of her delicious mouth, plunging his tongue into its honeyed recesses. God, she tasted sweet. And innocent.

Bloody dangerous. Stupid!

Her breathing raspy and irregular, she urged him nearer, her kisses that of a famished woman.

"Is Miss Katrina in her bedchamber?" Needham's voice cut through the passion fogging Nic's brain, and he tenderly clasped Katrina's hands, resting his forehead against hers.

"We must not be discovered like this. You'd be compromised."

She kissed his jaw then his chin.

"Let go, Kitty." Soundly castigating himself, Nic pried her fingers loose. Anyone could have come upon them.

Unless a promiscuous wanton, a woman in love with another man didn't kiss the way she had. Katrina most definitely wasn't the former. Was she the latter? How to find out?

"No, sir, I believe she's in the library with his grace," Osborne replied.

Katrina sprang away from him. Shaking her head, she slapped her palm across her mouth, her eyes huge and troubled. After sending a frantic gaze to the cracked door, she pointed to the desk, whispering,

"Your duchess prospectus."

"My *what*?" God's bones. It sounded like a treatise or dissertation.

"Shh." In one fluid movement, she slipped into the chair and seized the quill. "Open the ink. Be quick about it, and then stand there." She pointed to a spot beside her desk, a respectable distance away but which permitted him full view of the foolscap.

Nic swiftly did as she bid, taking a second to straighten one of the curls he'd mussed while kissing her. "There. No one will be the wiser."

"I shall," she muttered before stabbing the quill into the ink bottle. She raised her voice slightly. "What other qualifications do you require in a duchess, Your Grace?"

Pen poised, she affected an innocent air, and except for her rosy lips, no sign remained of the wanton who'd enjoyed his kisses but moments before.

Pity that.

He decided to test his newly developed theory. "Honesty and forthrightness."

A sound something similar to someone gargling

marbles or rocks escaped Katrina. She narrowed her eyes until Nic couldn't see her lovely, irate blue irises, but dutifully scratched the requirements. "A virtue desirable in a husband too, I should think."

"Aye. Always." Black mark for Domont, there.

"What else?" She didn't quite meet Nic's eyes, but fixed her gaze on his shoulder.

Thoroughly miffed. At him? Domont? Or herself?

Hmm, interesting, by Jove.

"Faithfulness." He folded his arms and winked. "Wouldn't do to be cuckolded before I have my heir and spare. Or worse yet, have another's by-blow forced upon the title."

Her eyes narrowed further, mere slits now, and Nic suppressed a grin. Oh, she hadn't liked that in the least. Another possible mark against Domont.

Enjoying himself far more than he ought to, Nic rested a shoulder against the shelf. All because Katrina had kissed him, which meant she couldn't be so very much in love with her major. Could she? She needed to realize that before she married Domont ... *If* she married him.

"Is that all?" Her clipped question contained more ire than defeat.

Good. Past time the spirited lass raised her hackles.

"Nay." Nic traced his scar. "I think she must know her own mind and not be afraid to speak it."

Katrina nodded, writing away. "Of course she must," she grumbled. "So a man can do whatever he bloody well wants anyway with no regard to her wishes or feelings?"

"My duchess would be my partner, my equal, my helpmate in all things." Not a typical philosophy, particularly for the nobility, but a woman treated with respect and equality made for a happier wife and a contented wife meant a pleasant marriage.

What do you care? You'll be at sea.

Not year-round, and he didn't wish his days at home to be hellish.

"Uh hum. I should like to see that." Katrina's features softened a fraction. "Anything else?"

"Aye."

Quill poised, she dared to meet his eyes.

147

Such turmoil churned in hers.

Nic spoke directly to her, reverently and sincerely, conveying what she'd mean to him if she were his duchess. "She should want, deserves, to be cherished and honored above all else."

Aye, Katrina should covet that, but his wife would know from the onset that the sea would always be his first love.

"Who should?" Needham marched into the library.

Either the man had a penchant for sniffing out his daughter in compromising situations, or he claimed blissful ignorance. A mite rude too, habitually intruding on others' conversations. Or dashed sly, and knew exactly what had transpired.

"Ah, working on your duchess list, Your Grace? I must say, I feel for you, Pendergast. A duke is a much sought after trophy." Needham waggled his eyebrows. "Too bad you don't have a lady in mind. It would surely save you a great deal of trouble."

"Indeed, sir. But I hope with Miss Needham's and Mrs. Needham's assistance to significantly lessen what could be a trying ordeal." Not the most romantic perception of marriage, but one necessitated by Nic's circumstances.

"Will we have the honor of your presence at the Granville's soirée tonight?" Needham eyed the books also sitting on Katrina's desk as he fingered his mustache.

Men with mustaches were forever fussing with them. Shave the thing and be done.

Nic looked at Katrina. "Should I attend?"

"I think so. Though it's a minor gathering, a few eligible young women will be present." Concern lined her usually smooth forehead. "But will your sisters be all right without you? It is their first night here, after all."

Naturally, she'd think of his sisters' welfare.

Would a devoted brother remain at home or pursue acquiring a bride?

"Yes, I believe so." Nic picked up a carved, gold-mounted, jade wax seal. He'd sent Aunt Bertie a similar ruby-encrusted lazuli stamp. "They've not spent much time with me as it is, and I know they were quite fatigued from the journey. I expect they'll wish to retire early."

"May I meet them first?" Katrina replaced the quill and smiled at Needham as he sauntered over.

"I'm sure they would like that." Nic wasn't sure of anything at the moment, especially the woman smiling serenely at her father.

Needham examined the diminutive list atop the desk. "Didn't get very far."

"His grace arrived but a short time ago, Papa." She studiously avoided looking toward Nic. "Besides, these things cannot be rushed."

"True, I suppose." Needham placed a hand on her shoulder. "I have news of Major Domont."

8

Katrina swallowed the nerves which launched to her throat. "Oh? Is that why I heard a carriage earlier? You've word from your man?"

Did she want to know what Papa had to say?

Yes. No. God help her, she really didn't know. She'd never been more conflicted in her life.

"It is, and I did." Gaze kind and unwavering, Papa's face revealed no hint of what he'd unearthed. "Peters sent a letter, but he's still in Stratford-Upon-Avon completing other tasks I asked him to attend to. For over a year, I've contemplated establishing a banking office there."

Katrina nodded distractedly. She loved Richard—wanted to be his wife. Didn't she? Why these reservations now? Because he hadn't been truthful with her, and a man who lied before marriage would most certainly do so afterward as well.

But what if he hadn't lied? If something unforeseen had arisen?

Then he should have written.

Common decency and courtesy, especially for someone he professed to love, required it. To leave her wondering, fretting ... A considerate man wouldn't do that...Which brought her right back to ... How important was she really to Richard?

And that sense-shattering kiss with Nic? Dear God. That scrumptiousness had sent her emotions spinning arse over teapot. Doubt raised its unnerving head, and not a dainty niggling misgiving, but a dragon-sized, fire-breathing uncertainty. In Nic's arms she'd felt ... cherished ... *home*.

Richard's kisses had never sent tingles pelting to her toes or made her forget where she was, her entire being focused on one thing. Nic's arms encircling her, his lips caressing hers, their tongues dancing and dueling. If Nic hadn't kissed her—fine, if *they* hadn't kissed—would she never have experienced such exquisiteness?

Why with him, a man she barely knew, and not Richard, who, until a few days ago, she'd been enamored of? Why with a man who'd made it clear he'd return to the sea, and therefore couldn't offer his heart to a woman, only his title and all that went with it?

Papa cleared his throat and ended Katrina's woolgathering.

"I'll excuse myself." Nic bowed, and after giving her an unfathomable look, quirked his delicious mouth and took his leave.

Wiping her damp palms on her gown, she stood. Somehow, perusing Nic's duchess qualifications while her father informed her whether she was to marry after all seemed ...well ...bizarre.

She cocked her head, still unable to read Papa's expression. "Well? Have I been jilted?"

His mouth hitched up on one side, and he withdrew a letter from his inside pocket. "Domont sent a note for you, and says he'll call in a day or two. There's been a change in his circumstances."

She arched her brows high before veeing them in bewilderment. "A change in his circumstances? Whatever does that mean? I suppose he might have resigned his commission, but why?"

"You'll have to read his letter to find out, Kitty." Papa extended the missive.

She accepted the letter and stared at Richard's bold scribbling. He had awful penmanship. The seal hadn't been broken either, which meant Papa hadn't read the letter as was typical.

"Shall I leave you alone?" Concern and uneasiness battled for supremacy in her father's warm gaze. "Or I can stay, if you prefer."

"You'll know the contents soon enough. You might as well stay." Katrina stepped to the window and, after breaking the seal, read the short missive.

My Dear Miss Needham,

Hmph. Back to Miss Needham, was she?

Afraid Papa might read the letter first perhaps? Or had the anonymous lady on Richard's arm brought about the formality?

Forgive me for my continued absence and for not writing sooner. Please believe me when I tell you I've thought of you daily, and as soon as I've dealt with the matters that have detained me, I shall call and explain everything in full.

There has been a dramatic change in my circumstances, and once you are made aware, I am sure you will extend me your forgiveness.

Oh, really? Just like that? Somebody better have died, for she'd only accept that excuse for such inconsideration.

You may expect me within the next two days, and I hope that you will be home to accept me.

Ever Yours,

R

Not even his full name, but a flamboyantly looped R? No *Love* or *Affectionately Yours*?

Refolding the letter, Katrina frowned. Richard's letter told her little more than her father had already disclosed.

She faced Papa, his posture alert and slightly wary.

"Major Domont begs my indulgence for a little longer and expects to call soon. He confirmed his circumstances have indeed changed, but he didn't explain what that change was." She waved the letter, and it crackled with the abrupt movement. "We know little more than we did, other than to expect him to call soon."

And that peeved her, teeth-gnashingly vexed her, truth to tell. She didn't know a dashed thing more. Didn't know if he still planned on asking for her hand. Didn't know if she wanted him to. Richard's vague letter only raised more questions.

The mantel clock chimed the hour and, sighing,

she slid the paper into her desk drawer where she wouldn't be tempted to read it over and over again, trying to instill hidden meaning into his brief message. "I'm going to take bonbons to his grace's sisters before I dress for the party."

"Only the four of us will attend the soirée. Your brothers have returned to London, and Shona is indisposed." Papa's attempt at normalcy fell flat.

As did Katrina's. "I know. I bade them farewell this morning."

"Come here, Kitty." Papa held out his arms, and she rushed into his embrace. "These things have a way of working themselves out, my dear."

Not always happily.

She stood on her toes and brushed his cheek. "Thank you for sending Peters."

Papa kissed the top of her head. "You know you don't have to marry Domont. I'll refuse his offer if you have the slightest hesitation, and I think you do. Especially since a certain duke sailed into your life."

Cheeks heated, Katrina jerked her head up.

"Papa, do you know what you're saying? His

grace wants a convenient wife, someone to lend him respectability, help raise his sisters, and provide him an heir. He's not interested in love nor does he plan on forsaking his wanderlust. The sea is his passion, and he'll return to her in a few short years." She shook her head and angled toward the door, hugging her shoulders against the room's sudden chill. "We'd never suit, in any event."

Her father made a noise in his throat. "Why not, if I might ask? From my observation, you already esteem one another and get on better than many married couples."

"Yes, but I want a man to marry me because he loves me, passionately, first and foremost, above everything. I thought Richard did," she said, lifting a shoulder an inch. "Now, I'm not altogether certain he does, and I hate the suspicion that has tainted my affections and muddled my thoughts."

"I've never been as sure as you about your major, my dear, but I want your happiness, and if he is your choice, I'll honor it." As they left the library, Papa patted her shoulder. "We'll wait and see what Domont has to say for himself, but I would caution you—no, ask you, Kitty—to reject his offer if you are not absolutely certain you love him and that he's the right man for you."

She had been convinced he was, and now feared she'd been wrong—so very, wretchedly wrong. How could she trust her fickle heart? One day, Richard was all she could think about, and now, Nic invaded her musings far more than Richard ever had.

A few minutes later, bonbons in hand, she tapped on Daphne and Delilah's bedchamber door. A moment passed before the door edged open, and a clear green gaze peeked out the slight opening. Daphne or Delilah?

Raising the plate of treats, Katrina offered a genial smile. "I've bonbons Cook would like my opinion on. She's tried several new recipes, but before she serves them to our guests, she wants to make sure they're acceptable. Would you mind terribly tasting a few? I cannot possibly eat them all, else I'll become quite ill. I would so appreciate the help."

After glancing behind her, the girl offered a timid smile and nodded as she eased the door open further.

"That would be lovely, Miss Needham. We weren't often permitted sweets at Chamberdall Court."

"Ah, you know my name. Wonderful. But when we are alone, you may call me Katrina or Kitty." She swept into the room and peered 'round. "I see you've made yourselves at home."

They'd done no such thing. Everything remained in place, as if they were afraid to touch anything or use so much as a hairbrush. After setting the plate upon a table near the balconied window, Katrina put her hands on her hips and cocked her head.

"Let me see if I can figure out which of you is Daphne and which Delilah. You look remarkably alike, I dare say."

The girls, their faces winter-pale, peered at her, their eyes wide and uncertain.

"You are Daphne." Katrina pointed to the girl who'd answered the door.

Though she stood barely taller than her sister, Daphne's hair glistened redder, and she'd begun to blossom into a young woman. Still retaining a child's thin figure, and her eyes sea green rather than emerald like her sister's, Delilah appeared the more bashful.

Katrina rotated her finger to indicate the younger girl. "And you are Delilah."

They nodded, but said nothing, although their hungry gazes strayed to the treats more than once.

Katrina retrieved the plate and, after kicking off her slippers, climbed onto the nearest bed. She patted the sunny coverlet. "Come. Join me."

The girls exchanged worried looks, and Daphne tossed a ginger-colored braid over her shoulder. "Is it allowed? Miss Tribble scolded us for mussing the bedclothes after we made our beds, and we were always made to sit straight in our chairs lest we wrinkle our gowns."

They weren't permitted to play? The unfortunate darlings.

"Of course it's permitted, and you don't even have to make your beds here, though I'm sure the maids will appreciate the gesture if you want to continue."

"She's much nicer than Miss Tribble," Delilah whispered to her sister.

"I bet Miss Tribble was a crotchety old battle axe,

wasn't she? I suppose tree-climbing and hide-and-seek weren't permitted either.

"No, miss," Daphne affirmed.

"Swimming? Archery? Blind Man's Bluff? Hot chocolate with clotted cream in bed on cold winter nights?"

Both girls shook their heads vehemently.

Katrina folded her knees beneath her and studied the assorted delicacies before selecting one. "Probably smelled of garlic and moldy cheese, farted in your presence, and snuck all the sweets for herself too."

A musical giggle escaped Delilah before she slapped a hand over her mouth and looked around ashamedly.

Katrina wiggled her eyebrows, holding her chocolate confection. "Now, do I have to eat all these sweets myself? I shall grow as tubby as Percival."

At that, both girls laughed and jumped onto the bed, still wearing their slippers. They'd about finished the entire plate when a single rap echoed at the door. Daphne shifted, likely to slip off the bed, but Katrina stilled her with a gentle hand to the girl's arm.

"Come in," Katrina called.

The door whooshed open to reveal a dashingly handsome Nic in evening black, his sandy hair slightly damp. He must have made a hurried trip to the tailor's, for he wore the height of fashion, down to his shoes. She rather preferred his tatty clothing and scuffed boots. His crisp cologne carried to her, and she stared through her eyelashes as he bowed to his sisters.

They'd scrambled off the bed and stood beside it, heads lowered and hands clasped.

Humor danced in his eyes as he bestowed a kind smile on the girls. "Did I hear giggling just now?"

"You did." Katrina lifted the near empty plate. "Would you care for the last two confections, Your Grace?"

"Indeed." He plucked both from the tray and popped the bonbons into his mouth, one right after the other. As he chewed, his gaze roved the tidy chamber. "What have you ladies been up to?"

"Getting acquainted. I've learned Daphne and Delilah's favorite colors, that they've never been taught to ride or swim or permitted a pet, and they both aren't terribly fond of beets or peas. Oh, and we all have a terrible sweet tooth."

Nic chuckled, wrinkling his nose. "Can't stand beets myself, especially pickled ones, and we'll need to remedy the pet oversight the instant we're settled at Chamberdall Court."

His sisters remained silent, their slender frames tense, prepared for chastisement.

Katrina firmed her mouth, not at all pleased how Nic's sisters cowered before him. After edging off the bed, she wrapped an arm around their shoulders. "Girls, your brother is a kind man. You needn't fear him. The moment he learned your mama and brother had died, he rushed to England to be with you. He wants you to feel safe and cared for."

Such gratitude filled Nic's expressive eyes that her belly jolted peculiarly.

Daphne's and Delilah's leery green gazes—old Pendergast must've had green eyes—shifted to Nic before darting away.

"Miss Tribble said if we annoyed the new duke, he'd make us walk the plank, and sharks would gobble us alive," Delilah whispered, her lower lip trembling and shoulders shaking as she buried her damp face in Katrina's waist.

Daphne scooted nearer too. "She also said you hated us because we're bas ... bastards and you had to leave the sea to take care of us."

Katrina tightened her embrace on the terrified girls, a wholly unladylike growl exploding from her. "Oh, I'd like to tell that evil dragon a thing or two. What a foul, lying, despicable—"

Nic folded to a knee before his sisters and took one of their small, white hands in his big, calloused palm. He scrutinized their anxious faces, so much tenderness in his that Katrina's eyes welled.

He loved them. Even though never permitted to be part of their lives, he loved them.

"Miss Tribble lied, Daphne and Delilah. I have wanted to know you since you were born, but it wasn't allowed. You're more important than my ship or the sea, and I wish us to be a family, along with my Aunt Bertie. I would like it very much if you would call me Nic too."

He flashed Katrina a rakish smile, and this time, all her insides quivered like jelly.

"And Miss Needham is helping me find a wife, so that you have a big sister to love you soon I would very much like it if you would also agree to help me with that, for my duchess must love you as much as I do."

Delilah looked between Katrina and Nic, her pale face scrunched. "Nic, you should marry Kitty, and have babies, at least five or six, and we can be one big family together."

"What a splendid idea." He quirked a tawny, mocking brow, and still on his knee, scooped Katrina's hand into his palm—warm and rough and wonderful. "What say you, Kitty, love? Would you take this sea-scoundrel-turned-duke, his adorable sisters, a sweet aunt, and make our family complete?"

9

An hour later, and still fuming, Katrina stalked the paneled corridor, holding her wrap, fan, and reticule in one hand and her sapphire blue skirt in the other. Why she'd elected to wear her betrothal gown tonight rather than at the Wimpletons' ball, she refused to examine closely.

Balderdash.

She'd worn it because she wanted to see the look on Nic's face when he saw her in it, even if she was mad as Hades at him.

Though he'd been playacting when he'd proposed, his sisters had thought him quite serious.

His unabashed grin still taunted—the devil.

"Dratted bore."

She might as well have told them their brother intended to ship them off to a boarding school in Switzerland, such disappointment shadowed their faces when Katrina explained she'd given her word to marry another. Well, she had, even if second thoughts now plagued her. Richard should be the first to know she meant to put an end to their relationship.

The realization cramped her lungs, and she faltered to a stop before a charming painting depicting a picnic.

My God. She *had* made that decision, though she couldn't say precisely when she'd come to the conclusion that marrying him would be a monumental mistake. But she had.

Relief didn't engulf her, but rather a tender, aching sort of sorrow. Katrina had worshiped Richard, had wanted to love him, until a certain oversized swashbuckler prompted her to examine her feelings closely. Too dashed closely. Truthfully, her pride stung far more than her heart ached at Richard's callousness and continued absence. Admitting herself capable of such shallowness chafed, but she'd never shied away from her faults.

When Richard came to call, she'd release him from his promise, and afterward reluctantly focus on fulfilling her foolish commitment to Nic. Of the tasks, the last would be the more difficult. Speaking with Richard was an unpleasant, but necessary obligation. However, finding Nic a bride? That she was loath to do.

Oh, the scheme had been a grand notion at the onset, but marching eligible misses beneath the nose of a man she harbored a *tendre* for ... that would take strength of character she wasn't altogether positive she possessed.

She'd given her word, however, and for his sisters' sakes, she would see the chore done. Afterward, she'd cry off men for a goodly while until she learned to control her feelings rather than have them governing her.

Before descending the stairs, Katrina took another bracing breath. She could do this—smile and pretend all was well. She'd introduce Nic to potential brides and refuse to acknowledge that each time she did, she'd bleed a little inside. And even being fully aware he married for convenience and would leave his wife for the sea one day didn't help ease the gloom shrouding her.

"Ah, there you are, my dear. I was about to come up and see what had delayed you." Mama, resplendent in an emerald and gold gown, smiled as Osborne helped her into an ermine-lined, gold velvet mantle.

A few feet away, Papa and Nic chatted quietly, but at Mama's comment, both shifted their attention to the stairs.

Why did Nic have to be so deucedly attractive? Have such a powerful physique? Be such a caring, gentle brother and nephew? Katrina would never be able to look upon other men without finding most pale, puny, and selfish in comparison.

His appreciative scrutiny traveled from Katrina's hair to her silk-covered toes then made the reverse journey, his kissable mouth bending into a sensual smile. Even with her parents gazing on, her traitorous body responded wantonly, heat radiating from her toes to eyebrows, with all manner of interesting sensations in between.

Descending the remaining stairs, she dropped her gaze and made a pretense of unfolding her wrap until her face cooled, and the fluttery, wobbly, puckering business calmed.

"A vision as always," Papa said and winked. He placed Mama's hand on his arm and guided her toward the door, obligating Nic to assist Katrina with her wrap.

Had Papa done that on purpose?

"You look exquisite." Nic brushed her arms with his fingertips, and a shiver stole across her, puckering the skin along her arms. *So do you.* He held her shoulders for a moment, whispering into her hair. "Am I forgiven for my earlier idiocy? That was a deuced awful way to propose."

She couldn't stay angry at the charming scoundrel and angled her head, meeting his contrite gaze. "Nic, your sisters thought you were serious."

Was she horribly foolish for wishing he had been? That he didn't love the sea more than he ever could a woman? Should she tell him about her decision not to marry Richard? What difference would it make?

Nic winked and gave her an enigmatic smile as he offered his arm. "Maybe I was. You'd make the perfect duchess."

Before she could unstick her tongue, he whisked her out the door, down the stairs, and into the waiting carriage.

Little besides banal weather or horseflesh conversation took place on the short ride to the Granvilles'. Nic sat beside Papa and politely answered the questions her parents put to him, but he seemed disinclined to talk. More than once, she felt his astute gaze on her.

Katrina kept her focus outside, even though darkness cloaked the view. As the carriage rumbled to a stop before the Granvilles' manor house, she filled her lungs with a bracing pull of air. Into the fray. Head up, smile in place, emotions firmly stowed.

"Are you ready, Your Grace?" Mama slanted her head toward the brightly lit house. "Your first foray into Society as a nobleman. Keep to us, and allow Hugo or me to make introductions. Katrina can help you choose which ladies to request a dance from and the ones you'll wish to avoid." Her tone dryer than paper, she muttered, "There are several."

Phoebe Belamont and her monstrous bosoms for one.

"Thank you," Nic murmured as he stepped from the conveyance and swept the carriage-lined drive a cursory glance. "Not too large a crush, I hope."

Nervous? Katrina subdued her twitching lips. Her brave privateer captain was terrified of venturing into the marriage mart. She almost felt sorry for him. Almost.

Once again, Papa escorted Mama, leaving Nic and Katrina to trail them. How had her parents come to trust him in such a short period? Her confounded lips jerked again. Well, he wasn't likely to pounce upon her or kiss her in full view of all, more was the pity.

Their earlier kiss had been quite the loveliest experience of her life. If she concentrated hard, she could still feel Nic's soft lips moving on hers. Katrina firmed her hold upon his arm as much in support as she enjoyed his muscles bunching beneath her fingertips, even through her gloves and his clothing.

"If you're not confident of your dance skills, don't

feel you must partner anyone tonight, Nic. I'll stay and help offer excuses. We should work out some sort of code too, so that I can let you know which ladies would suit and which won't."

Too bad he wasn't wearing a sword. He would need a weapon to fight the women off. She tightened her grip on her fan. The accessory might do in a pinch to discourage any overly aggressive misses. A grin threatened. Why, yes. She'd simply spend the evening holding her fan over her left ear, a polite way of telling them to trot along.

He's mine.

He wasn't, and couldn't ever be.

"Much obliged, but I believe I can manage a waltz without disgracing myself completely or crushing my partner's toes." He shot her a rascally grin. "How do I know you won't say all the ladies don't suit?"

"I'm not the jealous sort." Until now. Katrina sent him a sideways peek, admiring his bold and slightly imperfect profile. "Do you have time for a dance lesson tomorrow? Perhaps we could include your sisters as well. I'm sure they'd enjoy it."

"Aye, I've time, and I'm sure Daphne and Delilah would be thrilled to take part." A wry half-smile quirking his mouth, he dipped his head, his attention trained on the elegantly attired guests openly staring as he and Katrina entered. Or pretending not to behind half-lowered lashes or fluttering fans.

"This is a *minor* gathering?" Nic's nonplussed expression met with a soft giggle.

"Oh dear. News of the newly titled Duke of Pendergast's attendance must have preceded you. Mama probably accepted on your behalf. I hope you don't mind the attention, but a duke is a rarity at our simple, country events."

Momentarily taken aback by the sizable crowd, Katrina searched for her parents. Ah, there they were, greeting their ecstatic hostess. Through the open ballroom doors, music floated into the entry as the musicians warmed up. Dancing would commence soon.

Nic made a rough, affirmative sound in his throat before placing his hand atop hers resting on his forearm and returning the occasional cordial head tilt. His gaze tender, he murmured, "Thank you for being so kind to my sisters. They are quite taken with you already, as am—"

"Your Grace!" Mrs. Granville plowed across the parquet floor, towing her two pretty, *unattached* daughters. Her husband followed at a more sedate pace, wearing a bemused expression.

"Mama might have mentioned you sought a wife," Katrina muttered, surrendering her wrap. Good God. Half of Richmond milled about. How was she to manage all these ladies?

"Brace yourself," she muttered.

Nic gave a single, short nod, evidently assuming she spoke to him.

Entirely wrong. She'd meant the encouragement for herself.

"Your Grace," Mrs. Granville purred, sinking into a deep curtsy, promptly parroted by Regina and Abigail. "Please permit me to introduce my lovely daughters."

And so it begins.

Several moments passed as introductions were made to one gushing guest after another, and Nic took to his ducal role with such finesse and aplomb, Katrina wanted to applaud. He didn't need lessons at all. Likely his captaincy role had prepared him to some degree. From the corner of her eye, she caught sight of Phoebe Belamont gliding in their direction, a brazen invitation in her siren's gaze.

Botheration.

At that moment, Nic's gaze touched Katrina, and he must have noticed her disquiet. He offered a partial bow to those surrounding him. "Please excuse me. I hear a waltz beginning, and Miss Needham has promised me the first dance."

Fibber.

Surely Katrina's admiration showed in her delighted smile as she accepted his proffered arm, and he led her away from the disappointed misses and their equally frustrated mamas.

"Smoothly done, Your Grace. Phoebe's in such a froth, she looks like she swallowed slugs." Katrina's smile slipped a fraction. "You shouldn't be wasting a waltz on me, though."

"It's hardly a waste to snatch the most beautiful

woman present for the first dance. I'd say it's selfish, but as the highest ranking peer present, I suppose it's my due."

His patronizing tone and devilish wink earned him another smile, this one shyer.

Nic swung her onto the dance floor, his steps unpracticed, yet his natural grace apparent in his fluid movements and the ease with which he fell into the rhythm. "And I hope to convince you to allow me the supper dance as well. I seem to recall that only two dances are permitted unless a couple is married or betrothed, otherwise I'd claim every dance."

Katrina's heart soared foolishly, and she permitted him to edge her nearer.

Unwise, and oh, so dangerous. And delightful.

Nevertheless, she marshalled her resolve rather than melting into his muscular arms and permitting the music, the magical moment, *the man*, to make her forget their purpose tonight. She eased her chin upward, all too aware of the gazes trained on them. "People will assume we've formed an attachment, which rather defeats the purpose of you attending, does it not?"

"What say we call tonight our night to enjoy each other? We both have other obligations, but your kiss this afternoon tells me you're not any more impervious to me than I am to you." Nic rubbed his thumb over her ribs, and a delicious frisson shook her entire body.

Definitely not impervious.

He lowered his head, his intoxicating cologne enveloping her senses. "Next time, we can focus on responsibilities and commitments, but for tonight, I would pretend that you are mine, Katrina. What say you? Will you give me this night?"

I'd gladly give you a lifetime.

His thighs brushed hers as he nudged her gently, his tawny head much too close for propriety, his heated attention equally scandalous. "Will you? Please?"

He rasped the last hoarsely, but with such sincerity, her resolve melted away. His intense jade gaze probed hers, and Katrina found herself nodding, wanting to be his with everything in her being, no matter the consequences, even if it ended in heartbreak.

And how could it not?

"Yes. For tonight." And tomorrow, and the next

day, and the next.

A ragged sigh escaped him. "It will have to be enough."

It would never be enough.

The music ended, and Katrina reluctantly stepped away from Nic, instantly bereft without his strong arms holding her. Collecting her flustered thoughts, she curtsied. He didn't need dance lessons any more than he required instruction on comportment.

Blast Miss Sweeting for a job well done.

From the hopeful gazes directed his way from a handful of lovely young ladies, wholly suitable young ladies too, he wouldn't need her help to find a wife either.

"Would you like some ratafia?" He spoke over the sudden buzz circling the room and a commotion beyond the entrance.

Katrina looked up and smiled. "Yes. I'm quite thirsty."

They passed a cluster of young misses, including the Granville sisters, all chattering like magpies.

"A duke *and* a marquis in attendance tonight. Oh,

I may swoon." Abigail clutched her hands to her flat chest, closing her eyes dramatically.

Regina, her eyes round and shiny, nodded. "We'll be the envy of all Richmond. I do hope I dance with them both."

"So I have competition tonight." Laughter danced in Nic's eyes. "I'm quite put upon. I thought I was to be the center of attention. Who is this usurper marquis?"

Katrina shrugged. "Trust me, you are, and I haven't a clue who the marquis is. He must be an acquaintance of an invited guest."

Near the ballroom entrance, Mama motioned for them to join her and Papa. Actually, Mama gestured quite forcefully, a strained smile upon her face, while Papa, always more subdued, simply gave a beckoning nod. "Your Grace, my parents summon."

Were they miffed she'd danced with the duke?

"Is it me, or do they look a trifle disconcerted?" Nic steered her past several young bucks, who quickly averted their lustful perusal when he gave them a darkling glower.

My, that was nice. She could get quite used to a champion. "They do appear a bit tense."

As they wended their way to her parents, Nic smiled and nodded affably, earning him approving looks. He'd taken to this duke business like a seasoned sailor.

Once they reached her parents, her mother looped her arm through Katrina's. "My dear, you should know—"

"There he is, the Marquis of Maitland," a matron whispered behind her fan to her google-eyed crony.

Katrina glanced over her shoulder, straight into Richard's brown eyes, and gasped. "Blast and damn."

Taller than most everyone present, Nic searched behind Katrina for the source of her upset. A slender, swarthy fellow tastefully dressed in all black, save his crisp neckcloth, strode toward them. A path opened before him, and the room settled into a taut silence.

Domont.

Nic knew without being told who the striking fellow was. A marquisate certainly qualified as a change in circumstance but didn't excuse his not contacting Katrina.

Maitland's inquisitive gaze raked Nic before dismissing him, and he settled his attention on Katrina once more. He bowed, lifting her hand. "Miss Needham."

"Major. That is, my lord." Remarkably composed, Katrina dipped into a slight curtsy.

Maitland smiled and addressed the Needhams. "Please forgive me for not informing you sooner, but matters took time to settle. I am in mourning, and it would be most improper to remain, but it is urgent I speak with Miss Needham."

"You may call tomorrow." Expression steely, Needham offered the major ... er ... Maitland no succor.

A tight smile bending his mouth, Maitland peered around before stepping nearer. "I cannot. I must return home immediately. Things are in chaos there, but I didn't think a letter to Miss Needham would suffice. I should like to explain, if permitted. Osborne told me I might find you here."

Maitland couldn't keep his eyes off her, and Nic balled his fists. The dastard ignored her for weeks then inherited a title and came round? For a few minutes? What did he expect? She'd fall at his feet weeping? Throw herself into his arm with undying declarations of love?

Maitland had robbed Nic of his one night—his *only* promised night—with Katrina, and the urge to pummel the man, though unjust, overwhelmed.

This afternoon, his impulsive, bumbled proposal had been heartfelt. The timing and execution ... not terribly romantic. Fine, as romantic as a ship grounding on a reef during a typhoon. Nic had finally admitted that he wanted Katrina more than his ship, sailing, adventures and, damn it all, he'd waited too bloody long to tell her.

But above all else, he wanted Katrina's happiness, even if it meant he'd lost her to Maitland.

Maitland wasn't the interloper, Nic was, though it galled him to his fancy new shoes.

Katrina drew herself up and boldly met the curious gazes of those lurking nearby. "Papa, please give our excuses to the Granvilles and call for the carriage. Matters such as this are best settled in private, I think." She angled to face Nic. "Please don't feel compelled to leave on our account. The carriage can be sent for you later."

"No, I shall depart as well. I wish to look in on my aunt. She wasn't feeling well earlier when I peeked in on her."

Maitland frowned, his confusion evident. "Your aunt? Are you staying with the Needhams?"

Nic inclined his head. "Yes."

Think of that what you will.

Papa stepped forward. "Maitland, may I present, Dominic, the Duke of Pendergast, formerly Captain St. Monté? Your Grace, his lordship, Richard, the Marquis of Maitland, formerly Major Domont of His Majesty's Army."

"Ah, a captain in His Majesty's service." Maitland, the damned handsome cull, flashed Katrina a charming smile, though she appeared unaffected.

Given the feminine whispers and titters, she might have been the only female present under fifty who wasn't agog.

"No, his grace was ... is a commissioned privateer." A decidedly naughty smile tipped her pretty mouth when several ladies gasped. "A very, *very* successful privateer."

Well, perhaps not two verys' worth, still Nic summoned a rakish grin and nodded. "Indeed."

A few minutes later, they piled into the Needhams' carriage, Maitland squeezed between Nic's and Needham's larger forms. With every jolt in the road, Nic dug his elbow into Maitland's side. He'd bet his best rum Needham did the same on the other side.

"I say, old chap," Maitland grumbled after a particularly nasty jab.

"Beg pardon," Nic muttered, nearly choking on a laugh when Katrina's mouth twitched before she gave a dainty cough into her gloved hand.

Minx.

Maitland attempted trivial conversation, but when his efforts met with one word answers or vague noises, he reverted to silence

Still silent, everyone tracked into the house, and Osborne, wise servant, had a fire burning brightly in the drawing room along with a cold repast. "Water's on for tea. I shall bring a tray at once," he said, gathering their outerwear.

Curled on an armchair, Sir Pugsley slept, twitching every now and again in his sleep.

"I need something stronger than tea." Maitland gestured to the liquor cabinet. "May I?"

"By all means," Needham agreed, helping himself to a finger's worth too.

Nic could use a tot. A whole bloody bottle, truthfully.

Damn Maitland for appearing when he had. Nic had almost convinced himself to propose to Katrina again tonight. Properly this time. Then she could choose between him and Do—Maitland. At least then Nic would have tried to win her, even if she'd rejected his offer. She would've known he loved her, loved her so all-consumingly, he'd sell *The Weeping Siren* and never captain a ship again.

He hesitated at the drawing room's entrance. This was private family business. "I'll bid you good evening."

Katrina's eyes rounded a fraction, and she opened her mouth then snapped it shut, her lashes lowering as she shifted her attention to the fire. "'Til the morrow, Your Grace."

"I must say," Maitland said a distinctly peeved tone to his voice, "I'm not altogether keen on some fellow I don't know—a privateer to boot— residing beneath the same roof as my intended. Will somebody please explain to me how that came to be?"

10

"It's really not your concern, Richard, but suffice it to say, my parents extended his grace, his sisters, and his aunt an invitation to stay with us for a period. He is newly titled too, and I'm sure you of all people can appreciate the difficulties a sudden change in circumstances creates." Katrina poked the fire, more for something to do than any need to encourage the flames. "Mama, Papa, might I have a few minutes alone with his lordship?"

Richard—a lord. That had taken her unawares—totally flabbergasted her, truth be told.

Her parents exchanged a telling look.

Mama kissed Katrina's cheek and squeezed her hand. "I'll check in with you before I retire."

"Of course, my dear." Papa picked up Sir Pugsley, and, after leveling Richard an unreadable look, followed her mother from the room, leaving the double-doors cracked a respectable distance.

Katrina replaced the poker before facing Richard and folding her arms. The irritation she'd kept buried bubbled ever gradually upward. "So, you're a marquis now. I suppose congratulations are in order. I wasn't aware you were in line for a title."

Richard took a long pull from his second glass of brandy.

She scrunched her brows. Had he always drunk so freely?

He finished the spirit in one gulp and, setting the glass heavily on the table, cocked a smile. "My cousin held the title, and a fortnight ago, influenza took his life along with his heir's."

"I am truly sorry for your loss, Richard, but why didn't you contact me and tell me? I would certainly have understood your delay in returning." She waved her hand in the air before planting both hands on her hips. "You were seen out of uniform in Stratford-

Upon-Avon with a woman. A pregnant woman, I might add. I didn't know what to think but the obvious."

"I know, darling, but it's a mite more complicated than simply resigning my commission and inheriting the title." He combed his hand through his hair, a gold signet ring glinting on his little finger. "The woman is, was, the marchioness, and we were leaving her solicitor's office."

"She's in the family way, and she lost her husband and son? How utterly tragic." Remorse for her suspicious musings bathed Katrina.

Richard eyed the crystal decanter wistfully before his mouth edged upward. "Certainly for her, but not for me, you must agree."

"How can you take pleasure in her circumstances, Richard?" Katrina barely managed to keep her jaw from crashing into her chest. Who was this cold-hearted mercenary man? He'd kept this side of his character well-hidden. "Wait, if she's expecting, you can't be positive the title is yours yet."

"That's why I had to dally at Stonewater House, to see what the babe's sex was." He grinned fully then, a skin-prickling show of teeth, and practically crowed as he sauntered toward her. "A girl, born last night. A scrawny, red-faced, ugly, wrinkled thing. I told Amanda, she's the marchioness, I'd permit her and the infant to stay on for a month or so until she found other accommodations."

Katrina gasped and, taking a reflexive step backward, extended a palm to ward off his advance. "You turned her out? A grieving widow who's just given birth? My God, how could you be so heartless? So cruel?"

His dark brows dove together. "For you, my love. I didn't want you to have to share your new home, especially as newly-weds. Amanda has family. Don't fret about her and the child."

He tried to take Katrina in his arms, but she spun away, and he scowled.

"For me? No, for you. *You* didn't want to share your home with her." Putting the sofa between them, she clenched its carved mahogany top. "I would *never* have required her to leave, most especially under these tragic circumstances."

"Well, if it means so much to you, then of course Amanda can stay, although it may be a trifle awkward. We were pledged before she scampered off to Gretna Green and married my cousin." Bitterness dripped from every clipped syllable.

"Good God, and you didn't think I needed to know you'd been betrothed once already?" Arms folded, Katrina tapped one foot's toes rather than throw something at him.

"I told you I was estranged from my family." He eyed the brandy snifter longingly again. "The subject wasn't something I cared to discuss."

"Not even with the woman you professed to love?" Secrets before marriage never boded well afterward.

Richard wrinkled his forehead, his eyes slightly narrowed for an instant before pride lightened his countenance, and he pointedly changed the subject.

"Stonewater House is a grand old place, Katrina, though she needs updating. Think of the fun you'll have refurbishing the manor to your taste. Your dowry will help enormously, but unfortunately, it won't be sufficient for everything Stonewater needs. The estate has been rather neglected. But I'm confident your father will aid us. After all, you are his daughter, and he dotes on you."

Shaking her head once, not positive she'd heard him correctly, Katrina examined Richard's face. Had he always been this scheming, or had his new position so swiftly corrupted him? "Tell me something, Richard. If I'd been poor, from a family of humble means with no social standing, would you still have pursued me?"

He laughed and scratched his jaw. "But you aren't, and you don't, so the point is moot, isn't it? True, I'd prefer aristocratic blood in your pedigree." *Like a blasted hound or horse*? "But your beauty and family wealth offset the deficiency."

"Deficiency?" Oh, the bloody ... knave. Katrina gritted her teeth and stalked to the doors. "This conversation has been most enlightening. And since we're being honest with one another, I should tell you that I decided *before* I learned of your new status that I wouldn't marry you."

"You cannot be serious." His hands propped on his hips, confusion, disbelief, and anger paraded across Richard's face in quick succession. "You love me ... and I ... adore you too."

The last he sputtered. As an afterthought. Adore, not love? Most telling.

"Oh, I assure you, I am." She pushed a door open further. "Now, please see yourself out."

"I'll do no such thing." Shooting a swift, edgy glance at the doorway, he enunciated each softly spoken, ire-filled word. "The marquisate is nearly bankrupt. I need your dowry to pay for the improvements ... and a few debts I owe."

"That is not my concern."

"You cannot renege on your word." Prowling in her direction, he pointed and sneered. A demanding tyrant had replaced her good-natured, charming major.

Katrina jutted her chin up a notch despite the unease churning in her stomach.

"I most certainly can. There was never an official betrothal announcement. In fact, you haven't even asked Papa for my hand." Where was Papa? Had he retired? Osborne ought to be nearby. Surely someone lurked in the corridor. "You'll have to find another wealthy woman, God help her."

"Don't think I can't," Richard said, arrogance lending him an unbecoming air. "I've already been approached, but I wanted to do the honorable thing by you. Amanda would have me still."

Katrina jerked her hand toward the opening. "Please go. Thank God, I discovered your true character before we married. And to think, I really believed I loved you. I've been such a stupid, blind fool."

Richard flinched and swallowed audibly.

"You truly don't love me any longer?" Pain darkened his eyes, and he sucked in a long breath. Finally, he aimed his gaze at the floor, scrubbing a hand across his forehead. He made a noise, half snort and half caustic laugh. "And I suppose you think yourself in love with Pendergast? I didn't take you for a fast chit, Katrina."

The barb didn't strike home as he'd intended. She *was* in love with Nic.

"I now know what real love is, and what you and I

shared was not pure, unselfish, sacrificing adoration." Tears burned behind her eyes nonetheless. Bidding farewell to her first love, even if he'd turned out to be a feckless, selfish cawker, hurt. She raised her head and met his gaze square on. At one time, she'd lost herself in his eyes' warmth and devotion. No longer.

Breaking their gaze, he gave one short, sharp nod.

"Goodbye, Richard," she whispered thickly, her throat constricted with relief and regret.

Silent and neck bent, he strode from the room. A few moments later, the entry door thudded shut, and she released the breath she held.

Richard was gone. Out of her life for good. A week ago, she'd been sure she'd grow wrinkled and gray with him.

"I suppose I ought to tell my parents I'm not getting married after all." Yet her feet wouldn't move. "I'll probably wind up a daft, bonbon-munching spinster with a parlor full of fat, indulged dogs."

On cue, Sir Pugsley trotted in and, after snuffling around her skirt, looked up hopefully, his bum wiggling in excitement.

Katrina bundled the dog into her arms, kissing his fawn-colored head as she wandered to the sofa. Sighing, she sank onto the cushion before kicking her slippers off, shutting her eyes, and resting her head. She scratched behind Sir Pugsley's stubby ears.

"I believe I shall reserve my affections for you in the future, good sir. At least I'm sure you love me, and I needn't fret you'll leave me or break my heart."

"Then there's no hope for me?"

Katrina jerked upward so swiftly, she launched poor Sir Pugsley off her lap.

He yelped and turned offended button eyes on Nic, still wearing his evening attire.

What on Earth had Nic meant by that?

"Oh, Pugsley. I'm sorry. Come here." She held out her hands and wiggled her fingers. "I didn't mean to hurt you. I was startled."

Nic rescued the affronted animal, but instead of passing him to Katrina, he cuddled the dog as he sank onto the sofa beside her. Stretching his muscled legs before him, and running his long fingers over Pugsley's haunches, Nic cut her a sidelong look.

"Well, Kitty? Is there?"

"I ..." She clamped her lower lip between her teeth. Precisely how much had he heard? "I take it you saw Richard leave?"

"Aye." He crossed his ankles. "Concerned for your safety, Osborne fetched me from the library. He suggested a privateer might be more skilled at ridding the house of unwanted guests than an aging majordomo or your father."

"Barehanded?" She peered pointedly at Nic's hands as he petted Sir Pugsley, contentedly curled onto his thighs.

He lifted a shoulder and shifted the dog onto the sofa.

"Your major ... marquis might have been an army officer, but I sincerely doubt he'd eagerly go a round with me." Nic brushed his rough fingers across her cheek before trapping her hand in his, his gaze so loving, it stole her breath. He pressed a hot kiss to her knuckles before turning her hand over and kissing her palm. "You still haven't answered me, Kitty, love. Do I have a chance with you? Even the remotest one?"

"You do," Katrina whispered, her focus on his mouth. Lord, how she wanted to taste his lips again. "More than a remote one, actually."

"Thank God." Joy lit his face, and he scooped her onto his lap, burying his face in her neck. "I was terrified, more terrified than when I was captured by pirates, that you'd say no."

Sir Pugsley gave them a disgusted glance and jumped to the floor, where he resumed his nap.

Katrina leaned away. "You were captured by pirates? Real pirates?" She touched his scar. "Is that how you came by this?"

"No, this was the result of another battle, but enough of this talk. I want to talk about us, our future." He dropped a kiss onto her parted mouth, and she cupped his head, pressing her lips to his.

A deep, gravelly groan echoed deep in his throat, and Nic tilted her into his arms, pillaging her mouth, his tongue exploring—teaching her this new form of sensual play.

Katrina met each stroke of his velvety tongue, squirming to press nearer.

A hard bulge nudged her bum, and he rotated his hips upward.

"See what you do to me?" He pulsed against her bottom before tenderly pressing his forehead to hers.

Clutching him to her, she pressed a fervent kiss to his jaw. "You do the same to me."

"God, I love you, so desperately, so absolutely, and this vulnerability terrifies me, Kitty. I never expected love, didn't believe it was real, but each time I saw you, spoke to you, I became more captivated until nothing, no one, mattered as much as you. And the awful emptiness, the burning ache ripping me apart when I thought you belonged to another ..."

"Oh, Nic." She cupped his face, brushing his lips with hers, conveying all the adoration welling in her heart. "I was such an idiot."

He shuddered against her. "Tell me you love me too. That you'll marry me, be with me always? I want to fall asleep with you wrapped in my embrace, and wake in the morning the same way."

"I do love you, and will marry you, even though I know someday you'll return to the sea. I'll take the time you can give me and be blissfully happy, grateful for every moment." She laid her head against his broad chest, listening to his strong heart beating, and a tear escaped her. Even a day without him, let alone months, would be utterly unbearable, but oh, how sweet his homecomings would be. "And when you're sailing round the world, those memories will keep me warm until I'm in your arms again."

"I'll not leave you." Gently nudging her chin upward with his bent forefinger, Nic searched her face. "How can I leave my heart?"

Tears of joy crept over her cheeks. "You love the sea."

"I love you more, endlessly, abundantly, incomparably more. I'll sell *The Weeping Siren*, take to this duke business, and we'll raise a family, a whole passel of children to keep my sisters company." He rested his chin atop her head and chuckled. "I'm truly under your spell, and I confess, it's wondrous."

"Don't sell your schooner. I've always wanted to sail to different parts of the world. Perhaps she can be converted into a merchant ship? I know women are discouraged onboard, but could you make an exception for me once in a while, or is that asking too much?" Katrina angled away from him, giving him a flirtatious smile.

"Kitty, love, I'd do anything for you." He gathered her near, pressing his cheek against hers. "Because you've thoroughly and completely tamed this scoundrel's heart."

Epilogue

April 1819
Atlantic Ocean West of England

"Look, Nic." Katrina leaned over the schooner's rail and pointed to a water spout off the starboard side. "Is that a whale?"

Wrapping his arms around her from behind, Nic spoke into her hair. "It is. Watch closely. Those are humpbacks, and they swim in pods. They're migrating right now."

Before he finished speaking, two more whales surfaced.

"They're magnificent," she said, leaning into his strong embrace.

"Indeed." He kissed the crown of her head and splayed his fingers over her stomach.

"What do you think Aunt Bertie and your sisters are doing right now?" The three had taken to each other like bees to honey, and Chamberdall Court resounded with their laughter. Quite frequently, Aunt Bertie instigated some antic, most recently, teaching Daphne and Delilah to make jam tarts. For days afterward, Cook scolded about the mess they'd made in *her* kitchen.

Nic chuckled, his breath warming Katrina's head. "Probably into some sort of mischief, if I know my aunt. I still cannot fathom she'd been hoping for years to bring us together."

Katrina giggled. "That certainly explains why she regaled me with titillating tales of your adventures each time I visited, was thrilled when I agreed to help you find a bride, and why she didn't fuss when you moved her to our house."

"Crafty old bird." Affection laced his voice, and she sighed in pure contentment.

The sun dangled low on the western horizon, the

sky a myriad of yellow, peach, and burnished hues. Soon, they'd make their way to the captain's cabin for dinner. Anticipation sluiced her as an altogether different kind of hunger welled.

Trailing her fingers across his sturdy hands clasped at her middle, Katrina arched her neck to peek at him, and he promptly slid his hands beneath her cloak and cupped her breasts. She bit her lip against a moan when he tweaked her turgid nipples. "Perhaps we might watch the sunset from your ... our cabin?"

Gads, she sounded wanton.

They would reach England in a few days, and Nic would step into his ducal role full-time. This journey, a belated wedding trip to the tropics, was his farewell voyage. She'd protested that he couldn't forsake sailing, but he'd been adamant, especially when she'd revealed her delicate condition.

"Aye, and perhaps we'll work up an appetite for our supper beforehand." Nic turned her until she faced him and, amidst his crew's hoots and catcalls, kissed her soundly. Nic grinned as he looped her hand through his crooked elbow. "Cease your disrespect, or

I'll toss your sorry arses in the hold for the night."

"Aye, aye, Cap'n," echoed round the deck, followed by a chorus of laughter.

"They adore you, Nic. Are you sure you want to give this up? Won't you regret it?"

"No. This was my life before I gave you my heart." He opened the cabin door and waited for her to enter before closing the strip and shoving the bolt home. "Now, Kitty, love, I want to make a new life with you." He bent and kissed her flat stomach. "And this little one, and the others to follow."

Dear God, she loved this rugged, unpolished man. Unfastening the frogs at her throat, she meandered to the impressive bed dominating the cabin. After tossing her cloak on a nearby chair, she turned her back, smiling coyly over her shoulder. "And what do privateers do to the women whose hearts they capture?"

In four long strides, Nic crossed to Katrina. He scooped her into his arms and, after laying her on the coverlet, slid her skirts up her thighs to her waist. "They love them, until the breath leaves their body, and afterward, ever into eternity."

About the Author

USA Today Bestselling, award-winning author, COLLETTE CAMERON pens Scottish and Regency historicals, featuring rogues, rapscallions, rakes, and the intelligent, intrepid damsels who reform them.

Blessed with fantastic fans as well as a compulsive, over-active, and witty Muse who won't stop whispering new romantic romps in her ear, she lives in Oregon with her mini-dachshunds, though she dreams of living in Scotland part-time.

You'll always find dogs, birds, occasionally naughty humor, and a dash of inspiration in her sweet-to-spicy timeless romances®.

Her motto for life? You can't have too much chocolate, too many hugs, too many flowers, or too many books. She's thinking about adding shoes to that list.

Explore **Collette's worlds** at
www.collettecameron.com!

Join her **VIP Reader Club** and **FREE newsletter**.
Giggles guaranteed!

FREE 3-BOOK STARTER LIBRARY: Join Collette's The Regency Rose® VIP Reader Club to get updates on book releases, cover reveals, contests and giveaways she reserves exclusively for email and newsletter followers. Also, any deals, sales, or special promotions are offered to club members first. She will not share your name or email, nor will she spam you.

http://signup.collettecameron.com/theregencyrose

Follow Collette on BookBub
https://www.bookbub.com/authors/collette-cameron

From the Desk of Collette Cameron

Dearest Reader,

When I created Katrina's character in **Heartbreak and Honor**, I did so intending to write her story as one of the Waltz with a Rogue novels. And, Major Domont *was* going to be her hero. I bet he still hasn't forgiven me for making him the villain instead.

However, after I decided on the title, **To Tame a Scoundrel's Heart**—with a little help from my fabulous VIP Reader Group—a different kind of hero popped to mind. A sexy scoundrel privateer-turned-duke!

The chemistry between those two from the instant they met on the page drove the story along. At the risk of offending my other heroes, Captain Dominic St. Monte, is my favorite so far! I hope you fell in love with him, because I did.

Please consider telling other readers why you enjoyed Katrina and Nic's story by reviewing it at Amazon, Goodreads, Apple, or Barnes & Noble. Not only do I truly want to hear your thoughts, reviews are crucial for an author to succeed. **Even if you only leave a line or two, I'd very much appreciate it.**

So, with that I'll leave you.

Here's wishing you many happy hours of reading, more happily ever afters than you can possibly enjoy in a lifetime, and abundant blessings to you and your loved-ones.

Collette Cameron

A Kiss for Miss Kingsley
A Waltz with a Rogue, Book One

Can a beautiful spinster trust love again? Especially with the rouge who broke her heart the first time?

Caution: This humorous historical Regency romance contains a dashing, pessimistic rogue, a strong-minded heroine with a temperament as fiery as her red hair, an audacious aunt who says precisely what she thinks, and an uppity villainess who gets her comeuppance at last.

Olivia Kingsley didn't expect to fall in love and receive a secret marriage proposal two weeks into her first Season. However, one dance with Allen Wimpleton and her fate is sealed. Or so she thinks until her eccentric and ailing father announces he's moving the family to the Caribbean for a year. Distraught at her leaving, and unaware of her father's ill health, Allen demands she choose—him or her father.

Heartbroken at Allen's callousness, but thankful he's

revealed his true nature before she married him, Olivia turns her back on their love. The year becomes three, enough time for her broken heart to heal, and after her father dies, Olivia returns to England. Coming face to face with an embittered Allen, she realizes she never purged him from her heart, and once again the flames of passion ignite. But is it too late for their love?

Buy the first book in the Waltz with a Rogue historical Regency romance series for a rousing, emotional, and romantic adventure you can't put down.

Enjoy the first chapter of
A Kiss for Miss Kingsley
A Waltz with a Rogue, Book One

A lady must never forget her
manners nor lose her composure.
~*A Lady's Guide to Proper Comportment*

London, England
Late May, 1818

"This is a monumental mistake."

God's toenails. What were you thinking, Olivia Kingsley, agreeing to Auntie Muriel's addlepated scheme?

Why had she ever agreed to this farce?

Fingering the heavy ruby pendant hanging at the hollow of her neck, Olivia peeked out the window as the conveyance rounded the corner onto Berkeley Square. Good God. Carriage upon carriage, like great shiny beetles, lined the street beside an ostentatious manor. Her heart skipped a long beat, and she ducked out of sight.

Braving another glance from the window's corner, her stomach pitched worse than a ship amid a hurricane. The full moon's milky light, along with the mansion's rows of glowing diamond-shaped panes, illuminated the street. Dignified guests in their evening finery swarmed before the grand entrance and on the granite stairs as they waited their turn to enter Viscount and Viscountess Wimpleton's home.

The manor had acquired a new coat of paint since she had seen it last. She didn't care for the pale lead shade, preferring the previous color, a pleasant, welcoming bronze green. Why anyone living in Town would choose to wrap their home in such a chilly color was beyond her. With its enshrouding fog and perpetually overcast skies, London boasted every shade of gray already.

Three years in the tropics, surrounded by vibrant flowers, pristine powdery beaches, a turquoise sea, and balmy temperatures had rather spoiled her against London's grime and stench. How long before she grew accustomed to the dank again? The gloom? The smell?

Never.

Shivering, Olivia pulled her silk wrap snugger. Though late May, she'd been nigh on to freezing since the ship docked last week.

A few curious guests turned to peer in their carriage's direction. A lady swathed in gold silk and dripping diamonds, spoke into her companion's ear and pointed at the gleaming carriage. Did she suspect someone other than Aunt Muriel sat behind the distinctive Daventry crest?

Trepidation dried Olivia's mouth and tightened her chest. Would many of the *ton* remember her?

Stupid question, that. Of course she would be remembered.

Much like ivy—its vines clinging tenaciously to a

tree—or a barnacle cemented to a rock, one couldn't easily be pried from the upper ten thousand's memory. But, more on point, would anyone recall her fascination with Allen Wimpleton?

Inevitably.

Coldness didn't cause the new shudder rippling from her shoulder to her waist.

Yes. Attending the ball was a featherbrained solicitation for disaster. No good could come of it. Flattening against the sky-blue and gold-trimmed velvet squab in the corner of her aunt's coach, Olivia vehemently shook her head.

"I cannot do it. I thought I could, but I positively cannot."

A curl came loose, plopping onto her forehead.

Bother.

The dratted, rebellious nuisance that passed for her hair escaped its confines more often than not. She shoved the annoying tendril beneath a pin, having no doubt the tress would work its way free again before evenings end. Patting the circlet of rubies adorning her hair, she assured herself the band remained secure. The treasure had belonged to Aunt Muriel's mother, a Prussian princess, and no harm must come to it.

Olivia's pulse beat an irregular staccato as she searched for a plausible excuse for refusing to attend the ball after all. She wouldn't lie outright, which ruled out her initial impulse to claim a *megrim*.

"I ... we—" She wiggled her white-gloved fingers at her brother, lounging on the opposite seat. "Were not invited."

Contented as their fat cat, Socrates, after lapping a saucer of fresh cream, Bradford settled his laughing gaze on her. "Yes, we mustn't do anything untoward."

Terribly vulgar, that. Arriving at a *haut ton* function, no invitation in hand. She and Bradford mightn't make it past the vigilant majordomo, and then what were they to do? Scuttle away like unwanted pests? Mortifying and prime tinder for the gossips.

"Whatever will people *think*?" Bradford thrived on upending Society. If permitted, he would dance naked as a robin just to see the reactions. He cocked a cinder-black brow, his gray-blue eyes holding a challenge.

Toad.

Olivia yearned to tell him to stop giving her that loftier look. Instead, she bit her tongue to keep from sticking it out at him like she had as a child. Irrationality warred with reason, until her common sense finally prevailed. "I wouldn't want to impose, is all I meant."

"Nonsense, darling. It's perfectly acceptable for you and Bradford to accompany me." The seat creaked as Aunt Muriel, the Duchess of Daventry, bent forward to scrutinize the crowd. She patted Olivia's knee. "Lady Wimpleton is one of my dearest friends. Why, we had our come-out together, and I'm positive had she known that you and Bradford had recently returned to England, she would have extended an invitation herself."

Olivia pursed her lips.

Not if she knew the volatile way her son and I parted company, she wouldn't have.

A powerful peeress, few risked offending Aunt Muriel, and she knew it well. She could haul a haberdasher or a milkmaid to the ball and everyone would paste artificial smiles on their faces and bid the duo a pleasant welcome. Reversely, if someone earned her scorn, they had best pack-up and leave London permanently before doors began slamming in their faces. Her influence rivaled that of the Almack's patronesses.

Bradford shifted, presenting Olivia with his striking profile as he, too, took in the hubbub before the manor. "You will never be at peace—never be able to move on—unless you do this."

That morsel of knowledge hadn't escaped her, which was why she had agreed to the scheme to begin with. Nevertheless, that didn't make seeing Allen Wimpleton again any less nerve-wracking.

"You must go in, Livy," Bradford urged, his countenance now entirely brotherly concern.

She stopped plucking at her mantle and frowned. "Please don't call me that, Brady."

Once, a lifetime ago, Allen had affectionately called her Livy—until she had refused to succumb to his begging and run away to Scotland. Regret momentarily altered her heart rhythm.

Bradford hunched one of his broad shoulders and scratched his eyebrow. "What harm can come of it? We'll only stay as long as you like, and I promise, I shall remain by your side the entire time."

Their aunt's unladylike snort echoed throughout the carriage.

"And the moon only shines in the summer." Her voice dry as desert sand, and skepticism peaking her eyebrows high on her forehead, Aunt Muriel fussed with her gloves. "Nephew, I have never known you to forsake an opportunity to become, er ..."

She slid Olivia a guarded glance. "Shall we say, become better acquainted with the ladies? This Season, there are several tempting beauties and a particularly large assortment of amiable young widows eager for a *distraction*."

Did Aunt Muriel truly believe Olivia don't know about Bradford's reputation with females? She was neither blind nor ignorant.

He turned and flashed their aunt one of his dazzling smiles, his deeply tanned face making it all the more brighter. "All pale in comparison to you two lovelies, no doubt."

Olivia made an impolite noise and, shaking her head, aimed her eyes heavenward in disbelief.

Doing it much too brown. Again.

Bradford was too charming by far—one reason the fairer sex were drawn to him like ants to molasses. She'd been just as doe-eyed and vulnerable when it came to Allen.

"Tish tosh, young scamp. Your compliments are wasted on me." Still, Aunt Muriel slanted her head, a pleased smile hovered on her lightly-painted mouth and pleating the corners of her eyes. "Besides, if you attach yourself to your sister, she won't have an opportunity to find herself alone with young Wimpleton."

Olivia managed to keep her jaw from unhinging as she gaped at her aunt. She snapped her slack mouth shut with an audible click. "Shouldn't you be cautioning me *not* to be alone with a gentleman?"

Aunt Muriel chuckled and patted Olivia's knee again. "That rather defeats the purpose in coming tonight then, doesn't it, dear?" Giving a naughty wink, she nudged Olivia. "I do hope Wimpleton kisses you. He's such a handsome young man. Quite the Corinthian too."

A hearty guffaw escaped Bradford, and he slapped

his knee. "Aunt Muriel, I refuse to marry until I find a female as colorful as you. Life would never be dull."

"I should say not. Daventry and I had quite the adventurous life. It's in my blood, you know, and yours too, I suspect. Papa rode his stallion right into a church and actually snatched Mama onto his lap moments before she was forced to marry an abusive lecher. The scandal, they say, was utterly delicious." The duchess sniffed, a put-upon expression on her lined face. "Dull indeed. *Hmph.* Never. Why, I may have to be vexed with you the entire evening for even hinting such a preposterous thing."

"Grandpapa abducted Grandmamma? In church, no less?" Bradford dissolved into another round of hearty laughter, something he did often as evidenced by the lines near his eyes.

Unable to utter a single sensible rebuttal, Olivia swung her gaze between them. Her aunt and brother beamed, rather like two naughty imps, not at all abashed at having been caught with their mouth's full of stolen sweetmeats from the kitchen.

She wrinkled her nose and gave a dismissive flick

of her wrist. "Bah. You two are completely hopeless where decorum is concerned."

"Don't mistake decorum for stodginess or pomposity, my dear." Her aunt gave a sage nod. "Neither permits a mite of fun and both make one a cantankerous boor."

Bradford snickered again, his hair, slightly too long for London, brushing his collar. "By God, if only there were more women like you."

Olivia itched to box his ears. Did he take nothing seriously?

No. Not since Philomena had died.

Olivia edged near the window once more and worried the flesh of her lower lip. Carriages continued to line up, two or three abreast. Had the entire *beau monde* turned out for the grand affair?

Botheration. Why must the Wimpletons be so well-received?

She caught site of her tense face reflected in the glass, and hastily turned away.

"And, Aunt Muriel, you're absolutely positive that Allen—that is, Mr. Wimpleton—remains unattached?"

Fiddling with her shawl's silk fringes, Olivia attempted a calming breath. No force on heaven or earth could compel her to enter the manor if Allen were betrothed or married to another. Her fragile heart, though finally mended after three years of painful healing, could bear no more anguish or regret.

If he were pledged to another, she would simply take the carriage back to Aunt Muriel's, pack her belongings, and make for Bromham Hall, Bradford's newly inherited country estate. Olivia would make a fine spinster; perhaps even take on the task of housekeeper in order to be of some use to her brother. She would never set foot in Town again.

She dashed her aunt an impatient, sidelong peek. Why didn't Aunt Muriel answer the question?

Head to the side and eyes brimming with compassion, Aunt Muriel regarded her.

"You're certain he's not courting anyone?" Olivia pressed for the truth. "There's no one he has paid marked attention to? You must tell me, mustn't fear for my sensibilities or that I'll make a scene."

She didn't make scenes.

The *A Lady's Guide to Proper Comportment* was most emphatic in that regard.

Only the most vulgar and lowly bred indulge in histrionics or emotional displays.

Aunt Muriel shook her turbaned head firmly. The bold ostrich feather topping the hair covering jolted violently, and her diamond and emerald cushion-shaped earrings swung with the force of her movement. She adjusted her gaudily-colored shawl.

"No. No one. Not from the lack of enthusiastic mamas, and an audacious papa or two, shoving their simpering daughters beneath his nose, I can tell you. Wimpleton's considered a brilliant catch, quite dashing, and a top-sawyer, to boot." She winked wickedly again. "Why, if I were only a score of years younger ..."

"Yes? What *would* you do, Aunt Muriel?" Rubbing his jaw, Bradford grinned.

Olivia flung him a flinty-eyed glare. "Hush. Do not encourage her."

Worse than children, the two of them.

Lips pursed, Aunt Muriel ceased fussing with her

skewed pendant and tapped her fingers upon her plump thigh. "I would wager a year's worth of my favorite pastries that fast Rossington chit has set her cap for him, though. Has her feline claws dug in deep, too, I fear."

Bride of Falcon

A Waltz with a Rogue, Book Two

When is love not enough?

Caution: This historical Regency romance contains an intrepid, spinsterish wallflower convinced she's unworthy of love, a wounded hero determined to persuade her otherwise, and a cunning villainess you'll hope gets her comeuppance.

After five Seasons, Ivonne Wimpleton has accepted she's an haute ton undesirable. Her only suitors are men desperate to get their hands on her marriage settlement. Guarded and aloof, and always a bit ungraceful, she's resigned herself to spinsterhood. She doesn't mind her fate since Chancy Faulkenhurst, the man who once held her heart, left for India without an explanation.

Six years later Chance returns to England physically and emotionally scarred. His love for Ivonne remains just as strong, and when he learns she must choose one of the degenerates who've offered for her, he's determined that none should have her but him. Except, not only is she infuriated he made no effort to contact her in all their years apart, in Chance's absence, his father arranged a marriage for him and fully expects Chance to honor the agreement.

Buy the second book in the Waltz with a Rogue historical Regency romance series for a rousing, emotional, and romantic adventure you can't put down.

Her Scandalous Wish

A Waltz with a Rogue, Book Three

A marriage offer obligated by duty; an acceptance compelled by desperation.

Caution: This Regency historical romance contains a jaded lord whom the ladies adore, a scarred spinster, willing to sacrifice everything for her dying brother, a feisty, portly cat, and an audacious aunt who say precisely what she thinks.

Scarred from a fire, at two-and-twenty, Philomena Pomfrett is resigned to spinsterhood. But to ease her dying brother's fretting, she reluctantly agrees to attend a London Season to acquire a husband. If she fails, when he dies, with no family and no money, her future is perilous. Betrayed once, Philomena entertains no notions of a love-match.

Newly titled, Bradford, Viscount Kingsley, returns to England after a three-year absence. When he stumbles upon Philomena hiding in a secluded arbor during a ball, believing she died in a fire he doesn't recognize his first love. Yet something about her enthralls him, and he steals a moonlit kiss. Caught in the act by Philomena's brother, Bradford is issued an ultimatum—a duel or marry Philomena.

Bradford offers marriage, but Philomena rejects his half-hearted proposal, convinced he'd grow to despise her. Then her brother collapses, and she's faced with marrying a man who deserted her once already.

Buy this third book in the Waltz with a Rogue Historical Regency romance series for a rousing, emotional, and romantic adventure you can't put down.

The Wallflower's Wicked Wager

A Waltz with a Rogue, Book Five

**He loved her beyond anything and everything—
precisely why he must never marry her.**

Caution: This book contains one devilish, seemingly irredeemable rogue, an on-the-shelf wallflower who dabbles in wicked wagers, an unexpected and most enticing swim in a lake, a villainess you'll want to shove into said lake, and a cast of captivating secondary characters with their own tantalizing romantic tales.

A wounded hero.

Love—sentimental drivel for insipid, weak, feckless fools.

Since an explosion ravaged Captain Morgan Le Draco's face and cost him his commission in the Royal Dragoons, he's fortified himself behind an impenetrable rampart of cynicism and distrust. Now destitute and shunned by the very society that once lauded his heroics, he's put aside all thoughts of marrying and having a family. Until he risks his life to save a drowning woman. At once, Morgan knows Shona's the balm for his tortured soul, but as a wealthy, titled noblewoman, she's too far above his humble station and can never be his.

An intrepid wallflower.

Love—a treasured gift reserved for those beautiful of form and face.

Scorned and ridiculed most of her adult life, Shona, Lady Atterberry believes she's utterly undesirable and is reconciled to spinsterhood. She hides her spirited temperament beneath a veneer of gauche shyness, until a strapping, scarred stranger saves her life, and she can't deny her immediate, powerful, and sensual attraction to him. Despite how ill-suited they are and innuendos that Captain Le Draco is a fortune-hunter, she cannot escape her growing fascination.

Two damaged souls searching for love.

Others are determined to keep them apart, and Shona is goaded into placing a wicked wager. One that sets her upon a ruinous path and alienates the only man who might have ever loved her. Is true love enough to put their pasts behind them, to learn to trust, and heal their wounded hearts?

For a heartwarming, inspiring story about the power of love, purchase your copy today of THE WALLFLOWER'S WICKED WAGER, the fifth book in Collette Cameron's romantic historical Regencies A Waltz with a Rogue series.

The Earl and the Spinster

The Blue Rose Regency Romances:
The Culpepper Misses, Book One

***Would you sacrifice everything save your family?
Even your virtue?***

Caution: This book contains one stern lord with a dark secret he wants kept at all cost, a beautiful spinster smarter than the average man, an endearing, portly Welsh Corgi known to pee on gentlemen's boots, and a passel of well-meaning sisters and cousins who find themselves in one conundrum after the other.

Brooke Culpepper resigned herself to spinsterhood when she turned down the only marriage proposal she'd likely ever receive to care for her sister and cousins. After her father dies, a distant cousin inherits the estate, becoming their guardian, but he permits Brooke to act in his stead.

Heath, Earl of Ravensdale detests the countryside and is none too pleased to discover five young women call the dairy farm he won, and intends to sell, their home.

Desperate, pauper poor, and with nowhere to go, Brooke proposes a wager. Heath's stakes? The farm. Hers? Her virtue. The land holds no interest for Heath, but Brooke definitely does, and he accepts her challenge. Will they both live to regret their impulsiveness?

Buy the first book of The Blue Rose Regency Romances: The Culpepper Misses historical series for a romping, emotional, and romantic adventure you won't want to put down.

Enjoy the first chapter of

The Earl and the Spinster

The Blue Rose Regency Romances:
The Culpepper Misses, Book One

Even when most prudently considered,
and with the noblest of intentions, one who
wagers with chance oft finds oneself empty-handed.
~Wisdom and Advice
The Genteel Lady's Guide to Practical Living

Esherton Green,
Near Acton, Cheshire, England
Early April 1822

*W*as I born under an evil star or cursed from my
first breath?

Brooke Culpepper suppressed the urge to shake

her fist at the heavens and berate The Almighty aloud. The devil boasted better luck than she. My God, now two *more* cows struggled to regain their strength?

She slid Richard Mabry, Esherton Green's steward-turned-overseer, a worried glance from beneath her lashes as she chewed her lower lip and paced before the unsatisfactory fire in the study's hearth. The soothing aroma of wood smoke, combined with linseed oil, old leather, and the faintest trace of Papa's pipe tobacco, bathed the room. The scents reminded her of happier times but did little to calm her frayed nerves.

Sensible gray woolen skirts swishing about her ankles, she whirled to make the return trip across the once-bright green and gold Axminster carpet, now so threadbare, the oak floor peeked through in numerous places. Her scuffed half-boots fared little better, and she hid a wince when the scrap of leather she'd used to cover the hole in her left sole this morning slipped loose again.

From his comfortable spot in a worn and faded wingback chair, Freddy, her aged Welsh corgi, observed her progress with soulful brown eyes, his muzzle propped on stubby paws. Two ancient tabbies lay curled so tightly together on the cracked leather sofa that determining where one ended and the other began was difficult.

What was she to do? Brooke clamped her lip harder and winced.

Should she venture to the barn to see the cows herself?

What good would that do? She knew little of doctoring cattle and so left the animals' care in Mr. Mabry's capable hands. Her strength lay in the financial administration of the dairy farm and her ability to stretch a shilling as thin as gossamer.

She cast a glance at the bay window and, despite the fire, rubbed her arms against the chill creeping along her spine. A frenzied wind whipped the lilac branches and scraped the rain-splattered panes. The tempest threatening since dawn had finally unleashed its full fury, and the fierce winds battering the house gave the day a peculiar, eerie feeling—as if portending something ominous.

At least Mabry and the other hands had managed to get the cattle tucked away before the gale hit. The herd of fifty—no, sixty, counting the newborn calves—chewed their cud and weathered the storm inside the old, but sturdy, barns.

As she peered through the blurry pane, a shingle ripped loose from the farthest outbuilding—a retired stone dovecote. After the wind tossed the slat around for a few moments, the wood twirled to the ground, where it flipped end over end before wedging beneath a gangly shrub. Two more shingles hurled to the earth, this time from one of the barns.

Flimflam and goose-butt feathers.

Brooke tamped down a heavy sigh. Each structure on the estate, including the house, needed some sort of repair or replacement: roofs, shutters, stalls, floors, stairs, doors, siding...dozens of items required fixing, and she could seldom muster the funds to go about it properly.

"Another pair of cows struggling, you say, Mr. Mabry?"

Concern etched on his weathered features, Mabry wiped rain droplets from his face as water pooled at his muddy feet.

"Yes, Miss Brooke. The four calves born this mornin' fare well, but two of the cows, one a first-calf heifer, aren't standin' yet. And there's one weak from birthin' her calf yesterday." His troubled gaze strayed to the window. "Two more ladies are in labor. I best return to the barn. They seemed fine when I left, but I'd as soon be nearby."

Brooke nodded once. "Yes, we mustn't take any chances."

The herd had already been reduced to a minimum by disease and sales to make ends meet. She needed every shilling the cows' milk brought. Losing another, let alone two or three good breeders...

No, I won't think of it.

She stopped pacing and forced a cheerful smile. Nonetheless, from the skeptical look Mabry speedily masked, his thoughts ran parallel to hers—one reason she put her trust in the man. Honest and intelligent, he'd worked alongside her to restore the beleaguered herd and farm after Papa died. Their existence, their livelihood, everyone at Esherton's future depended on the estate flourishing once more.

"It's only been a few hours." *Almost nine, truth to tell.* Brooke scratched her temple. "Perhaps the ladies need a little more time to recover." *If they recovered.* "The calves are strong, aren't they?" *Please, God, they must be.* She held her breath, anticipating Mabry's response.

His countenance lightened and the merry sparkle returned to his eyes. "Aye, the mites are fine. Feedin' like they're hollow to their wee hooves."

Tension lessoned its ruthless grip, and hope peeked from beneath her vast mound of worries.

Six calves had been guaranteed in trade to her neighbor and fellow dairy farmer, Silas Huffington, for the grain and medicines he'd provided to see Esherton Green's herd through last winter. Brooke didn't have the means to pay him if the calves didn't survive—though the old reprobate had hinted he'd make her a deal of a much less respectable nature if she ran short of cattle with which to barter. Each pence she'd stashed away—groat by miserable groat, these past four years—lay in the hidden drawer of Papa's desk and must go to purchase a bull.

Wisdom had decreed replacing Old Buford two years ago but, short on funds, she'd waited until it was too late. His heart had stopped while he performed the duties expected of a breeding bull. Not the worst way to cock up one's toes...er, hooves, but she'd counted on him siring at least two-score calves this season and wagered everything on the calving this year and next. The poor brute had expired before he'd completed the job.

Her thoughts careened around inside her skull. Without a bull, she would lose everything.

My home, care of my sister and cousins, my reasons for existing.

She squared her shoulders, resolution strengthening her. She still retained the Culpepper sapphire parure set. If all else failed, she would pawn the jewelry. She'd planned on using the money from the gems' sale to bestow small marriage settlements on the girls. Still, pawning the set was a price worth paying to keep her family at Esherton Green, even if it meant that any chance of her sister and three cousins securing a decent match would evaporate faster than a dab of milk on a hot cook stove. Good standing and breeding meant little if one's fortune proved meaner than a churchyard beggar's.

"How's the big bull calf that came breech on Sunday?" Brooke tossed the question over her shoulder as she poked the fire and encouraged the blaze to burn hotter. After setting the tool aside, she faced the overseer.

"Greediest of the lot." Mabry laughed and slapped his thigh. "Quite the appetite he has, and friendly as our Freddy there. Likes his ears scratched too."

Brooke chuckled and ran her hand across Freddy's spine. The dog wiggled in excitement and stuck his rear legs straight out behind him, gazing at her in adoration. In his youth, he'd been an excellent cattle herder. Now he'd gone fat and arthritic, his sweet face gray to his eyebrows. On occasion, he still dashed after the cattle, the instinctive drive to herd deep in the marrow of his bones.

Another shudder shook her. Why was she so blasted cold today? She relented and placed a good-sized log atop the others. The feeble flames hissed and spat before greedily engulfing the new addition. Lord, she prayed she wasn't ailing. She simply couldn't afford to become ill.

A scratching at the door barely preceded the entrance of Duffen bearing a tea service. "Gotten to where a man cannot find a quiet corner to shut his eyes for a blink or two anymore."

Shuffling into the room, he yawned and revealed how few teeth remained in his mouth. One sock sagged around his ankle, his grizzled hair poked every which way, and his shirttail hung askew. Typical Duffen.

"Devil's day, it is." He scowled in the window's direction, his mouth pressed into a grim line. "Mark my words, trouble's afoot."

Not quite a butler, but certainly more than a simple retainer, the man, now hunched from age, had been a fixture at Esherton Green Brooke's entire life. He loved the place as much as, if not more than, she, and she couldn't afford to hire a servant to replace him. A light purse had forced Brooke to let the household staff go when Papa died. The cook, Mrs. Jennings, Duffen, and Flora, a maid-of-all-work, had stayed on. However, they received no salaries—only room and board.

The income from the dairy scarcely permitted Brooke to retain a few milkmaids and stable hands, yet not once had she heard a whispered complaint from anyone.

Everybody, including Brooke, her sister, Brette, and their cousins—Blythe, and the twins, Blaike and Blaire—did their part to keep the farm operating at a profit. A meager profit, particularly as, for the past five years, Esherton Green's legal heir, Sheridan Gainsborough, had received half the proceeds. In return, he permitted Brooke and the girls to reside there. He'd also been appointed their guardian. But, from his silence and failure to visit the farm, he seemed perfectly content to let her carry on as provider and caretaker.

"Ridiculous law. Only the next male in line can inherit," she muttered.

Especially when he proved a disinterested bore. Papa had thought so too, but the choice hadn't been his to make. If only she could keep the funds she sent to Sheridan each quarter, Brooke could make something of Esherton and secure her sister and cousins' futures too.

If wishes were gold pieces, I'd be rich indeed.

Brooke sneezed then sneezed again. Dash it all. A cold?

The fresh log snapped loudly, and Brooke started. The blaze's heat had failed to warm her opinion of her second cousin. She hadn't met him and lacked a personal notion of his character, but Papa had hinted that Sheridan was a scallywag and possessed unsavory habits.

A greedy sot, too.

The one time her quarterly remittance had been late, because Brooke had taken a tumble and broken her arm, he'd written a disagreeable letter demanding his money.

His money, indeed.

Sheridan had threatened to sell Esherton Green's acreage and turn her and the foursome onto the street if she ever delayed payment again.

A ruckus beyond the entrance announced the girls' arrival. Laughing and chatting, the blond quartet billowed into the room. Their gowns, several seasons out of fashion, in no way detracted from their charm, and pride swelled in Brooke's heart. Lovely, both in countenance and disposition, and the dears worked hard too.

"Duffen says we're to have tea in here today." Attired in a Pomona green gown too short for her tall frame, Blaike plopped on to the sofa. Her twin, Blaire, wearing a similar dress in dark rose and equally inadequate in length, flopped beside her.

Each girl scooped a drowsy cat into her lap. The cats' wiry whiskers twitched, and they blinked their sleepy amber eyes a few times before closing them once more as the low rumble of contented purrs filled the room.

"Yes, I didn't think we needed to light a fire in the drawing room when this one will suffice." As things stood, too little coal and seasoned firewood remained to see them comfortably until summer.

Brette sailed across the study, her slate-blue gingham dress the only one of the quartet's fashionably long enough. Repeated laundering had turned the garment a peculiar greenish color, much like tarnished copper. She looped her arm through Brooke's.

"Look, dearest." Brette pointed to the tray. "I splurged and made a half-batch of shortbread biscuits. It's been so long since we've indulged, and today is your birthday. To celebrate, I insisted on fresh tea leaves as well."

Brooke would have preferred to ignore the day.

Three and twenty.

On the shelf. Past her prime. Long in the tooth. Spinster. *Old maid.*

She'd relinquished her one chance at love. In order to nurse her ailing father and assume the care of her young sister and three orphaned cousins, she'd refused Humphrey Benbridge's proposal. She couldn't have put her happiness before their welfare and deserted them when they needed her most. Who would've cared for them if she hadn't?

No one.

Mr. Benbridge controlled the purse strings, and Humphrey had neither offered nor been in a position to take on their care. Devastated, or so he'd claimed, he'd departed to the continent five years ago.

She'd not seen him since.

Nonetheless, his sister, Josephina, remained a friend and occasionally remarked on Humphrey's travels abroad. Burying the pieces of her broken heart beneath hard work and devotion to her family, Brooke had rolled up her sleeves and plunged into her forced role as breadwinner, determined that sacrificing her love not be in vain.

Yes, it grieved her that she wouldn't experience a man's passion or bear children, but to wallow in doldrums was a waste of energy and emotion. Instead, she focused on building a future for her sister and cousins—so they might have what she never would—and allowed her dreams to fade into obscurity.

"Happy birthday." Brette squeezed her hand.

Brooke offered her sister a rueful half-smile. "Ah, I'd hoped you'd forgotten."

"Don't be silly, Brooke. We couldn't forget your special day." Twenty-year-old Blythe—standing with her hands behind her—grinned and pulled a small, neatly-wrapped gift tied with a cheerful yellow ribbon from behind her. Sweet dear. She'd used the trimming from her gown to adorn the package.

"Hmph. Need seedcake an' champagne to celebrate a birthday properly." The contents of the tray rattled and clanked when Duffen scuffed his way to the table between the sofa and chairs. After depositing the tea service, he lifted a letter from the surface. Tea dripped from one stained corner. "This arrived for you yesterday, Miss Brooke. I forgot where I'd put it until just now."

If I can read it with the ink running to London and back.

He shook the letter, oblivious to the tawny droplets spraying every which way.

Mabry raised a bushy gray eyebrow, and the twins hid giggles by concealing their faces in the cat's striped coats.

Brette set about pouring the tea, although her lips twitched suspiciously.

Freddy sat on his haunches and barked, his button eyes fixed on the paper, evidently mistaking it for a tasty morsel he would've liked to sample. He licked his chops, a testament to his waning eyesight.

"Thank you, Duffen." Brooke took the letter by one soggy corner. Holding it gingerly, she flipped it over. No return address.

"Aren't you going to read it?" Blythe set the gift on the table before settling on the sofa and smoothing her skirt. They didn't get a whole lot of post at Esherton. Truth be known, this was the first letter in months. Blythe's gaze roved to the other girls and the equally eager expressions on their faces. "We're on pins and needles," she quipped, fluttering her hands and winking.

Brooke smiled and cracked the brownish wax seal with her fingernail. Their lives had become rather monotonous, so much so that a simple, *soggy*, correspondence sent the girls into a dither of anticipation.

My Dearest Cousin...

Brooke glanced up. "It's from Sheridan.

46875868R00146

Made in the USA
Middletown, DE
02 June 2019